"No one could find this probe unless they knew where to look."

Kathryn frowned. The probe was wedged into a cleft where the rock ledge curved under. "But how do we get it out?" She did not add what else she was thinking. *Without falling.*

"Good question," Jon said. "I don't want to climb down over the edge."

"That won't be necessary." As T'Lor knelt beside the Klingon, Fiona suddenly screeched overhead. It was the hawk's shrill warning of danger.

Everyone looked up, including the tethered riding animals they had left at the edge of the clearing. The *targ* raised his snout to test scent.

The *sehlat* yelped in pain somewhere in the woods.

A monstrous catlike animal with greenish brown fur and gleaming fangs burst out of the forest with an enraged roar. It charged toward them with unbelievable speed.

Kathryn dropped to one knee, prepared to spring aside. It was a futile exercise. They were all trapped on a ledge that ended in thin air on three sides.

There was nowhere to run.

Available from MINSTREL Books

STAR TREK®
VOYAGER™

STARFLEET ACADEMY®

THE CHANCE FACTOR

Diana G. Gallagher and Martin R. Burke

**Interior illustrations by
Jason Palmer**

A MINSTREL® BOOK

Published by POCKET BOOKS
New York   London   Toronto   Sydney   Tokyo   Singapore

A MINSTREL PAPERBACK *Original*

A Minstrel Book published by
POCKET BOOKS, a division of Simon & Schuster Inc.
1230 Avenue of the Americas, New York, NY 10020

A VIACOM COMPANY

STAR TREK is a Registered Trademark of Paramount Pictures.

ISBN: 0-671-00732-7

First Minstrel Books printing September 1997

10 9 8 7 6 5 4 3 2 1

Cover art by Michael Herring

Printed in the U.S.A.

To Betsey Wilcox,
who "skippered" the launch of the authors'
lifetime voyage together

STARFLEET TIMELINE

2264

The launch of Captain James T. Kirk's five-year mission, _U.S.S. Enterprise,_ NCC-1701.

2292

Alliance between the Klingon Empire and the Romulan Star Empire collapses.

2293

Colonel Worf, grandfather of Worf Rozhenko, defends Captain Kirk and Doctor McCoy at their trial for the murder of Klingon chancellor Gorkon.

Khitomer Peace Conference, Klingon Empire/Federation (_Star Trek VI_).

2323

Jean-Luc Picard enters Starfleet Academy's standard four-year program.

2328

The Cardassian Empire annexes the Bajoran homeworld.

2346

Romulan massacre of Klingon outpost on Khitomer.

2351

In orbit around Bajor, the Cardassians construct a space station that they will later abandon.

2353

Kathryn Janeway enters Starfleet Academy.

2355

Kathryn Janeway meets Admiral Paris and begins a lifelong association with the esteemed scientist.

2363

Captain Jean-Luc Picard assumes command of <u>U.S.S. Enterprise,</u> NCC-1701-D

2367

Wesley Crusher enters Starfleet Academy.

An uneasy truce is signed between the Cardassians and the Federation.

Borg attack at Wolf 359; First Officer Lieutenant Commander Benjamin Sisko and his son, Jake, are among the survivors.

<u>U.S.S. Enterprise</u>-D defeats the Borg vessel in orbit around Earth.

2369

Commander Benjamin Sisko assumes command of Deep Space Nine in orbit over Bajor.

2371

<u>U.S.S. Enterprise,</u> NCC-1701-D, destroyed on Veridian III.

Former <u>Enterprise</u> captain James T. Kirk emerges from a temporal nexus, but dies helping Picard save the Veridian system.

<u>U.S.S. Voyager,</u> under the command of Captain Kathryn Janeway, is accidentally transported to the Delta Quadrant. The crew begins a 70-year journey back to Federation space.

2372

The Klingon Empire's attempted invasion of Cardassia Prime results in the dissolution of the Khitomer peace treaty between the Federation and the Klingon Empire.

Source: <u>Star Trek</u>® <u>Chronology</u> / Michael Okuda and Denise Okuda
and <u>Star Trek</u>® <u>Voyager</u>™ <u>Mosaic</u>/Jeri Taylor

Chapter

1

Horrified, Cadet Kathryn Janeway stared at the bio-control panel in the ship's science lab. The containment field isolating the poisonous alien microorganism the team was assigned to analyze had just failed.

"Do something, Chov!" Mario Santori looked at the Tellarite in charge of the bioscan.

Cadet Chov placed his hand on his panel and froze.

"What happened, Tava?" Kathryn yelled at the Andorian cadet as she frantically keyed her board to discharge a lethal burst of high-intensity radiation. There wasn't time to wait for Chov to figure out a defense.

"A glitch in the power conduits interrupted the energy flow to the field and I—I didn't notice it right

1

away!" The Andorian girl's blue skin darkened to a deeper shade when she glanced at Kathryn's panel. "An eradication sweep! Are you crazy? We'll be killed!"

"We're dead anyway, Tava!" Chov snorted through his piggish nose. "I should have thought of a radiation sweep."

"At least the rest of the crew has a chance." Mario sighed heavily and continued to monitor the environmental status board. "It could be a lot worse. This corrosive critter is still confined to the lab—"

"Lab seals disintegrating," the flat computer voice said calmly. "Total failure in three seconds."

Kathryn didn't hesitate. She initiated the radiation sweep sequence.

"Seal integrity compromised."

The computer's blunt announcement hit Kathryn with a force more devastating than a phaser blast. She closed her eyes against the blinding glare of the radiation burst that neutralized all life in the lab—one second too late.

The airborne microorganism was loose in the ship.

Everyone on the *U.S.S. Lancaster* would die in less than thirty minutes. . . .

The memory of the *Lancaster* disaster burned in Kathryn's mind. She had failed—completely. How could she ever explain that she was responsible for the death of an entire crew to her father? Even if it *was* only a holosimulation. *Simple,* she thought dismally. She couldn't.

Urging Shawnee into a trot, Kathryn began to post with practiced ease. Moving up and down in the saddle to counter the bounce of the horse's brisk gait, she concentrated on the staccato sound of shod hooves on hard-packed ground. Horseback riding was one of many recreational activities Starfleet Academy provided for the cadets. Kathryn hadn't had time to visit the stables since arriving a few weeks before, but five minutes in the arena had convinced Lieutenant Commander Ralston that she was a competent equestrian. Not only had he given her permission to ride alone, he had asked her to ride Shawnee, a high-strung thoroughbred that was desperately in need of some exercise. Taking to the trails without Bramble was a painful reminder of the little dog's recent death, but a relaxing ride had always helped her sort through her problems back home in Indiana.

It wasn't working this morning.

Kathryn had hoped the hypnotic rhythm of the horse moving beneath her would numb her troubled mind, but nothing could distract her from the one thing she feared most—failure. But failing so miserably because someone *else* had made a fatal error was something she couldn't reconcile.

It was a mistake that would have killed all seventy-six people on the survey vessel—including her—if the situation had been real and not a simulated training exercise.

With a slight pressure on the reins, Kathryn brought Shawnee back to a walk as the bridle path turned in to the woods. The tall trees blocked the sun, dimming the light and creating gray shadows along the trail. The darker atmosphere suited her somber mood. She couldn't escape the sobering realization that one day she might *really* die because of another person's incompetence.

Even worse, Kathryn thought grimly, *what if an error in* my *judgment kills someone?* It was a possibility she couldn't accept, but one she had to face.

A shrill, panicked scream suddenly shattered the quiet tranquillity of the forest and broke through Kathryn's dismal reflections. Her reaction was instant and instinctive.

Pushing everything else out of her mind, Kathryn tightened her legs and her grip on the reins. The horse began to prance nervously, but she held him to a steady jog as she continued down the path and tried to pinpoint the direction of the cry and the sound of pounding feet. She saw a flash of green and gray dart through the dense foliage ahead and to her right. On the left, through the thinning trees, another rider in Starfleet red and black was riding furiously up an intersecting trail. The rider giving chase was a couple of hundred yards behind the runaway.

Realizing that she was closer, Kathryn pressed Shawnee into a controlled hand-gallop and plunged off the path into the trees. By angling through the woods, she could intercept the runaway long before the other rider caught up.

Leaning low over Shawnee's neck, Kathryn kept a sharp eye on the terrain in front of her. Running cross-country was dangerous for both her and the horse. A large branch could easily knock her out of the saddle, and if Shawnee stepped into a hole at this speed, he could break a leg. For the most part, the ground was clear and the trees were spaced far enough apart to maintain a fairly direct course.

Turning her face into Shawnee's neck to avoid being slapped by a branch, Kathryn looked up to see a large log ahead. She was already in position and moved her hands forward to prevent popping the horse's mouth as he sprang and extended his head over the barrier. Gathering Shawnee back when he landed, she looked to her left as the runaway rider squealed again.

"What on earth—" Kathryn blinked. Through a break in the trees, she saw a human boy wearing cadet gray clinging desperately to his saddle. But he wasn't riding a horse. He was mounted on a giant, four-legged, green—saurian? With three heads! It was small compared to the extinct Earth giants, she realized, but it was lithe and fast!

Recovering quickly from the shock of the bizarre and unexpected sight, Kathryn calculated her course and pace in relation to the 'saur that was racing through the woods. The reins on the bridle fitted to the center head were flapping freely on the crest of the long neck. Even if the boy got his panic under control, he still wouldn't be able to stop the animal. Ahead Kathryn could see the large meadow that separated the forested land from the Academy complex. If Shawnee could give her a burst of speed, she would break into the grassy expanse ahead of the charging lizard.

"Hang on, Castille!" a male voice bellowed.

Kathryn glanced back as her horse responded to her legs and thundered forward. The Starfleet officer was gaining on the runaway, but not fast enough. If the lizard wasn't stopped, it might charge straight into the congested Academy courtyards. A lot of people could be hurt.

The space between Kathryn and the runaway closed steadily. Then suddenly, all three heads jerked up and the creature shied to one side. Unprepared for the abrupt move, the rider fell off. Seeing the Starfleet officer jump from his horse and run to help the boy, Kathryn focused totally on the lizard.

As Kathryn had figured, Shawnee ran into the meadow slightly ahead of the 'saur. Not knowing how the horse would react if he got too close to an alien dinosaur with too many heads and an unfamiliar scent, Kathryn kept her distance and turned in a wide circle around the grassy field. Tired and riderless, the lizard didn't seem too anxious to get close to her and Shawnee, either. Rather than trying to charge past her, it followed a similar but tighter course in ever-diminishing circles.

Leading his winded horse, the Starfleet officer walked out of the woods with the boy just as the creature came to a stop. Kathryn reined Shawnee to face it. The 'saur stared back with six unblinking, yellow eyes. The horse snorted and she squeezed her legs to keep him from backing away. The man handed his reins to the boy and slowly approached. Kathryn had to keep the 'saur from running again until he reached it. When the lizard jumped to one side, Kathryn used

the dressage techniques she had never fully appreci-
ated to counter the move.

The Starfleet officer's eyes widened as Shawnee
sidestepped to block the lizard's path. Moving slowly
around to the front of the creature, he spoke softly
and extended his hand. As though sensing the futility
of its situation, the animal lowered its center head,
and the man grabbed the loose reins. He jumped back
as the left head tried to nip his shoulder. The right
head continued to stare at Kathryn.

With the runaway caught, Kathryn exhaled long and
hard and patted Shawnee soundly on the neck.

"That was the slickest piece of horsemanship I've
seen in quite a while, young lady. A very clever ma-
neuver, that circling."

"Thank you, sir." As hard as Kathryn strove to
excel, she was never comfortable responding to com-
pliments. "It works with runaway horses."

"And you weren't sure how your horse would feel
about getting too close to a three-headed dinosaur,
either."

"That was a concern, sir. Yes."

"Captain Holbrook. And you're Cadet—" The man
rubbed the underside of the trembling lizard's long,
pointed central snout, which seemed to calm it. The
left head took over the watch, while the right head
snatched a large grasshopper from the grass.

"Janeway, Captain. Cadet Kathryn Janeway."

"I'd shake your hand, but I don't want to upset
your horse or this Sehgal serpent again."

"That's quite all right, sir. I've got to get back to

the Academy for class and Shawnee needs to be cooled out. With your permission, sir."

"By all means." Nodding, Captain Holbrook dismissed her with a smile.

Inclining her head respectfully, Kathryn turned Shawnee back toward the woods. She resisted the urge to check the time until she was out of sight. It was later than she realized, but she couldn't race back to the stables. The horse was overheated and had to be cooled down before she put him away. If she didn't take the time to walk him back to the barn, she'd have to walk him when she got there.

And she still had to shower and change. It was also reasonably safe to assume that this would be one of those days her hair absolutely refused to behave.

Kathryn was dreading the debriefing that would no doubt focus on her team's inadequate and deadly performance in the alien-biota simulation.

And now—she was going to be late!

Chapter

2

"So good of you to join us, Cadet Janeway," Commander Roberts said coldly.

Closing the classroom door, Kathryn marched to her seat under the instructor's hard gaze. She hoped the flush of embarrassment burning her cheeks wasn't as red as it felt. Sliding into her chair, she realized that her three teammates were too preoccupied with their own problems to care about hers. At least Commander Roberts was debriefing the teams as individual groups. Having their poor performance rated in front of the whole class would be too much to bear.

"As I was saying," Commander Roberts went on. "All of you had opportunities to avert the biological contamination before, during, and after the containment field failed." He graced each of the cadets with a pointed stare. "One or two of those options might have saved *your* lives, too."

"What options, sir?" Stunned, Kathryn blurted out the question without raising her hand to be recognized. Commander Roberts chose to overlook it, but not because he was letting her off the hook.

"Why don't you tell me?"

Kathryn's mind reeled, but she couldn't just sit there like a total dunce and not respond to a direct question. "A secondary containment field—isolating the whole lab. Then the organism wouldn't have contaminated the rest of the ship before the radiation sweep killed it."

The instructor nodded. "Quite true. But you and your associates would still be dead."

"Not if we had been wearing e-suits." Kathryn paled, her voice dropping almost to a whisper. "Environmental suits would have saved us."

"But the organism was corrosive!" Chov rose out of his seat, his snout wrinkling with indignation. "I had already determined that it could degrade metals and plastics as well as organic substances on contact. It would have eaten through the e-suits just like it did the seals."

Kathryn breathed easier when Commander Roberts turned his probing attention on the Tellarite. "And just when did you arrive at that conclusion, Cadet?"

"Thirty-eight minutes after I began my analysis." Grunting curtly, Chov sat back down.

Mario's dark eyes narrowed. "But e-suits would

have protected us from the radiation sweep. The organism would have been neutralized before it compromised our suits."

"Yeah." Tava's antennae bobbed as she emphatically nodded her head. "And maybe Kathryn wouldn't have hesitated to initiate the sequence if she knew she wouldn't die."

Kathryn's head snapped around to stare at the Andorian. She wasn't angry. Tava had made a valid point and Kathryn couldn't avoid the implication. *Had* she hesitated for that one critical second that would have destroyed the organism before it escaped the lab and killed the crew?

"Don't blame Janeway, Tava." Chov's small beady eyes blazed. "We wouldn't have *needed* a radiation sweep if you had noticed the energy fluctuation and modified the power flow *before* it shut down the field!"

"But I—" Tava sputtered, then sagged.

Commander Roberts interrupted sharply. "I think you've all gotten the point."

"We have?" Mario scowled, bewildered.

Clasping his hands behind his back, the instructor began to pace. "*If* you had been wearing e-suits. *If* the interruption in power had been noticed. *If*, ladies and gentlemen, is the operative word. You have to consider all the 'ifs' in any situation, because the Chance Factor is always present. Always."

"Like Murphy's Law?" Kathryn asked. It was an ancient Irish saying her father liked to quote, claiming that Murphy was an optimist. "If anything *can* go wrong, it *will.*"

Commander Roberts smiled and the tension in the room eased. "In a way. The Chance Factor is a defining phrase for the fact that *nothing* is absolutely certain or predictable—including seals and containment fields and, most especially, alien organisms we know nothing about."

Kathryn nodded. "So we should have considered everything that could go wrong and then taken precautions against them—no matter how remote the possibilities."

"Yes," Commander Roberts said. "But even then, it's impossible to take everything into account. Starfleet's business *is* the unknown, and sometimes the unknown is deadly. But there are certain pitfalls we can *always* avoid."

"Like what, sir?" Mario asked.

"The *Titanic* is an ideal example. She was a great seagoing cruise ship that sank in the Atlantic Ocean on Earth in 1912 after hitting an iceberg. One thousand, five hundred twenty-three of her crew and passengers went down with her. Only seven hundred and five survived, even though it was a calm night with a flat sea."

"That's awful!" Tava shook her head in disbelief.

"How could that happen?" Chov's gruff manner softened.

The instructor took a deep breath. "The *Titanic* was built with double hulls, and the men who built her had the arrogance to believe that she couldn't possibly sink. And they convinced everyone else that nothing could take the ship down. Because of that assumption, the *Titanic* wasn't equipped with enough lifeboats for everyone."

Kathryn shifted uncomfortably, finding it hard to accept the senselessness of the *Titanic*'s fate. It was a tragedy that could so easily have been avoided.

"Arrogance and assumption are the prelude of disaster," Commander Roberts said in closing. "Dismissed."

Kathryn rose and headed for the door in a daze. *Arrogance and assumption.* How often was she *so* certain she knew the best solution or had the right answer. A scientific mistake could be just as fatal as a warp-core breach or a wrong command decision.

"Cadet Janeway!"

"Huh?" Kathryn blinked at Commander Roberts. "Sir?"

"Commander Brannon would like to see you in her office at fourteen hundred hours."

Kathryn's breath caught in her throat. She had not requested a meeting with her advisor. "Why, sir?"

"I'm sure she'll be happy to tell you." Commander Roberts glanced at his watch. "In about ten minutes."

As Kathryn hurried toward the administration building, she was sure that Commander Brannon was going to tell her what she had suddenly figured out for herself.

That she wasn't fit to be a Starfleet officer.

* * *

"At ease, Kathryn." Commander Brannon smiled kindly.

"Yes, sir. Ma'am. Uh—"

" 'Commander' will do nicely. Have a seat."

Kathryn sat—perched stiffly on the edge of the chair—as the gray-haired woman quickly scanned her padd.

"You're quite an accomplished young woman, Cadet Janeway. Tennis, diving, horseback riding. An impressive academic and athletic record at the Academy Institute. Vice-Admiral Janeway must be very proud of you."

Kathryn acknowledged the comment with a nod. Her father was so busy dealing with the Cardassian problem, she rarely saw him. Even so, she was convinced that she disappointed Edward Janeway more often than she made him proud, but there was no need to draw the counselor's attention to that.

"How do you feel about your team's performance in the bioemergency simulation yesterday?"

The question, which had nothing to do with what they had been discussing, was asked so casually that Kathryn answered without thinking. "Not very good, Commander."

"And why is that?" Commander Brannon folded her hands on her desk and leaned forward expectantly.

Blindsided! Disarmed by the reference to her father, Kathryn had walked right into her advisor's verbal trap. There was no way out but to answer honestly.

"I was responsible for the death of an entire crew because I didn't act fast enough."

"Were you the only one who made a fatal error?"

"No, sir!" Kathryn stiffened. "Cadet Tava didn't notice a power interruption that triggered the emergency. Chov was analyzing the organism and should have initiated the radiation sequence, but he didn't. So I did. And Mario Santori could have programmed a containment field for the lab, but he didn't do that, either. And none of us thought to wear e-suits as a precaution against the unexpected."

"What aspect of the exercise disturbs you the most?"

Kathryn almost shrugged, but caught herself. "Knowing that my life may depend on someone who doesn't know what they're doing. Or that *I* might make a fatal mistake. It's a toss-up."

Commander Brannon's expression remained composed as she made a note, then sat back. "Are you familiar with the *Kobayashi Maru* exercise for command-track cadets?"

"I've heard of it. The scenario is almost impossible to beat. Someone did once—a long time ago." Kathryn saw the advisor smile slightly, as though she knew more about the infamous test than she was willing or allowed to say. The *Kobayashi Maru* was like a secret ritual that people only mentioned in whispers.

The woman cleared her throat. "Yes, well . . . James T. Kirk aside, the scenario was designed to test emotional reactions to failure. Yesterday's biosim does the same thing. If a team solves one potentially lethal problem, it's presented with another, and then another. You had no hope of saving the *Lancaster* crew."

Kathryn frowned. "But Commander Roberts just told us we had options that *could* have averted the disaster."

"You did—to a degree. Wearing e-suits would have prolonged the inevitable, as would any one of several other measures you might have taken. The bioemergency simulation is the ultimate demonstration of the Chance Factor, but that isn't its only purpose."

"I see." Kathryn's mouth tightened. She felt betrayed by a simulation that was programmed to insure failure. How could anyone *pass* a failure test?

"I'll be blunt, Kathryn. Academy cadets are expected to strive for and achieve a level of excellence, but no one is perfect. No one. You've set unrealistic, and therefore self-defeating, expectations for yourself. And you have difficulty accepting anything less than perfection in others. Do you think that's a fair assessment?"

Kathryn nodded and lowered her gaze. She couldn't speak because of the lump in her throat.

"You have the potential to be a fine science officer," the commander continued gently. "The essence of exploration is the discovery of the unknown and, consequently, the handling of unpredictable situations. Starfleet officers have to be flexible in order to function effectively and they must be prepared to cope with the unexpected. You've certainly proven yourself capable in that regard."

Kathryn raised her eyes and met Commander Brannon's concerned gaze.

"But equally important, a good officer has to accept

and overcome his or her own imperfections and deal with the limitations of others." The woman hesitated, sighing. "And you do seem to have a problem with that."

Swallowing hard, Kathryn struggled to maintain an expression of calm reserve. The commander's observation was correct and she had no defense. She would just have to work harder to control her feelings and adjust her attitude.

"The sooner unsuitable cadets are weeded out of the Academy," the counselor said gravely, "the better for everyone, including those young people who must find a different direction for their lives. In your case, I'm convinced there's only one thing to do at this point."

Numb with disbelief, Kathryn braced herself. She was going to be kicked out of the Academy and Starfleet before she even got started!

Chapter

3

As Kathryn walked down the path toward the stables, she reviewed her discussion with Commander Brannon for the hundredth time since leaving her office yesterday afternoon.

To Kathryn's immense relief, she had not been asked to leave Starfleet Academy. Not yet, anyway. Based on her round-up of the stampeding lizard the previous morning, Captain Holbrook had requested that Kathryn be assigned to a feasibility study he was conducting on Diehr IV. Commander Brannon had granted the request because she thought that a change of scene and focus would do more to help Kathryn evaluate herself and her goals than a month of counseling.

Kathryn suspected that she had only been given a temporary reprieve. Her performance on Captain Holbrook's mission might very well determine whether or not her future included a commission in Starfleet. Still, rather than being depressed about the uncertainty of her status, Kathryn was more than prepared to meet the challenge.

And succeed. This isn't the first time I've had to deal with a difficult situation, Kathryn thought as she breathed deeply of the cool morning air. She had conquered tennis, which she had loathed at first, and figured out every physics problem her father had thrown at her, even when he was too preoccupied to notice or care. Adversity never got the best of her. Instead, it always seemed to spur her to greater effort. She had never heard of the planet Diehr IV, but she was determined to conquer it, too.

Kathryn hadn't questioned why Captain Holbrook wanted her to report to the stables. Starfleet didn't have a mounted division. She had assumed the captain used the facility for recreation like the cadets and had chosen the comfortable surroundings for their introductory talk. However, her high spirits and confidence took a sudden and unexpected plunge when she turned in to the stable drive. The courtyard was a chaotic scene of squawking, snarling, and hissing alien animals.

A small boy with dark hair and a leather bag slung over his shoulder was desperately trying to quiet the Sehgal serpent. All three heads were screeching.

"Easy, easy, Rayonica. Please. . . ." The boy didn't

pull on the reins when the huge saurian frantically backed up. The beast was twenty times heavier than the boy and he could not possibly control it with brute strength. He moved with the lizard instead.

Kathryn frowned, dismayed that Captain Holbrook had put a child in charge of a dinosaur. Curious, she had consulted her padd about Sehgal serpents last night before going to sleep. No catastrophe had occurred on Sehgal to wipe them out as it had on Earth. They looked like huge cold-blooded, reptilian lizards. Although the word "saur" in "dinosaur" meant "lizard," human scientists had long known that Earth's dinosaurs had evolved into warm-blooded creatures. The Sehgal serpent was warm-blooded and fairly smart, too. The large brain was located in a bony cavity between the shoulders where the necks connected with the body. One mind controlled all three heads, appendages that functioned like sensory arms. The animal was also high-strung, fast, and dangerous.

But apparently, Kathryn realized, her fears were unfounded. The boy closed his eyes and held out his hand. Shaking but calmer, the 'saur lowered its heads. Scratching the left and right chins, the boy nuzzled the center snout. All three heads *whuff*ed with contentment.

A slim Vulcan girl watched passively from the door of a small barn across the yard from the main stable. One of her hands rested on the head of a huge, shaggy creature Kathryn recognized as a Vulcan *sehlat*. Except for its long fangs, it looked very much like an Earth bear. The girl's other hand rested on the back of an Andorian *zabathu.* Tava had shown Kathryn a picture of the desert beast she used to ride. With its long legs and neck and wide feet, it resembled a camel without the humps. The *zabathu* had short white fur, blue eyes, and a silky, golden mane. Long golden hair flowed from the tip of its skinny tail—like a lion's. Except for flicking its tail, it seemed as unconcerned about the unruly dinosaur as its Vulcan handler.

Kathryn blinked as a commotion drew her gaze to the side of the smaller barn. A Klingon boy was tugging on a leash attached to an ugly horned creature with bristle hair that looked like a pig with a bad attitude. Another boy with a bumpy ridge running from his forehead over the top of his skull was trying to catch a gigantic black spider with nine-inch legs. The spider seemed intent on provoking the snarling pig-thing, and both boys were yelling at each other.

Kathryn's heart lurched. She had never seen a Klingon in person before. Although the Klingon Empire and the Federation had been at peace since the Khitomer accords of 2293, Klingons preferred to stay isolated from Federation society. With his long, tangled hair, ridged forehead, and uneven, protruding teeth, the boy looked just like the holopictures of Klingon warriors in her history references.

"If that hook spider of yours bites my *targ,* Endar, I'll roast it for dinner!" the Klingon roared with a ferocity that matched the *targ*'s frenzied snarl as it lunged at the spitting insect.

"Try it and *you'll* feel the sting of Talarian revenge, Thorn!" Stepping in front of the spider, Endar

scooped it into his arms and held it protectively against his chest.

A shiver of revulsion raced up Kathryn's spine. The Federation and the Talarians had been warring since they had first encountered each other. A race that kept spiders as pets demanded respect, but the presence of a sworn enemy was unnerving. *What have I gotten myself into?*

"Kathryn!" Captain Holbrook called from inside the barn. "Excuse me, T'Lor."

The Vulcan girl moved her animals aside as he stepped through the door. He was leading a heavy beast that looked like a skinny rhinoceros with a longer neck and narrower head. The animal's body was covered with hard, armored plates like an armadillo's. It had a horn on its forehead and three more down the crest of its neck like the *targ.*

Kathryn let out a long, discouraged breath as Captain Holbrook held up a hand for her to wait.

"Thorn! Come get your *sark,* please!"

Hauling the *targ* away from Endar, the Klingon took the lead shank from the captain. Kathryn started with surprise when Thorn smiled and rubbed the lumbering *sark* behind its rounded, fur-tufted ears. The animal grunted and groaned.

"Yes, Hov nej. It feels good, I know. Come on, Jup." Urging the *targ* to follow, the Klingon boy led the *sark* to a watering trough.

Endar came around the corner of the barn with the spider perched on his shoulder. Four of its eight, hairy legs were draped around his neck.

"Bring Ginjar out, would you, Endar?" Captain Holbrook asked as he waved Kathryn over. "I want everyone to meet the newest member of our expedition."

The Talarian boy did not glance at her as he turned toward the barn, but Kathryn heard a low, puttering noise coming from the spider that sounded like purring!

"Good to see you, Kathryn," the captain said as he extended his hand. Fine lines around his merry blue eyes crinkled when he smiled. "I suppose you're wondering what's going on here."

"Yes, sir." Smiling tightly, Kathryn prudently kept quiet. She sometimes spoke before she stopped to think, which didn't always endear her to her peers and superiors. Right now, she was in enough trouble.

"Come on. I'll explain while I give you the grand tour." Brushing a thick lock of blond hair off his tanned forehead, Captain Holbrook ushered Kathryn into the small barn. "What did Commander Brannon tell you?"

"Only that you were doing a study on Diehr Four."

"Actually, this mission is just a preliminary exercise. Whether or not I get funding to conduct a full-scale study depends on the results of the Diehr Four expedition." Captain Holbrook shrugged. "Investigating the potential applications of nontechnological resources is not high on Starfleet's list of priorities, I'm afraid."

"Nontechnological resources?"

"The official terminology for animals and all things primitive. Occasionally, Starfleet encounters emergency situations on worlds where cultural considerations or conditions prevent the use of standard, high-tech equipment and operations. I'm convinced that the animals used on different worlds during their preindustrial development can be put to effective use again—for rescues and preliminary surveys. That kind of thing."

"I see." To Kathryn's left, Endar put a halter on another unknown animal. A single, spiraled horn graced the space between its huge, green eyes. Covered in long, very fine silver hair, it held its head high on a long, slender neck. Even with six legs, two pair in back and one pair in front, Ginjar was as elegant as the spider was grotesque.

"A Talarian *t'stayan*," Captain Holbrook said softly. "Not terribly swift, but it can climb a cliff like a mountain goat. Better maybe. It's also exclusively bonded to one rider."

"I'll remember that." Kathryn nodded, noting that Endar still refused to look at her.

"Exactly why I wanted you on the team, Kathryn. Cadet Castille insisted on riding Rayonica even though Jon warned him the serpent wouldn't respond to physical control."

"How do you control it?" Kathryn asked curiously.

"No one but Jon Brezi can. He's a Betazoid. He formed a mental link with Rayonica on Sehgal. His father's a xenobiologist on the Federation survey outpost there."

As they continued down the center aisle, Captain Holbrook answered the question that was suddenly foremost in Kathryn's mind. How did she fit into this bizarre assembly of beast and handler?

"Cadet Castille's obvious lack of good judgment and respect for the unfamiliar made it necessary to replace him. I must admit, I didn't think I'd find someone who could step in at the last minute and do the job. But then you demonstrated an innate understanding of unpredictable animal behavior yesterday and solved that problem for me."

"Thank you, Captain."

"Diehr Four is a wilderness planet that doesn't have an indigenous intelligent species. For the mission's purposes, we'll invent a primitive population, though. I'm sure it'll be an exciting and challenging adventure for you."

Kathryn nodded, hoping her disappointment was not evident. She had grown up in a traditional community where families adhered to an old-fashioned, twenty-second-century lifestyle. With an aptitude for science and a fascination for technology, Kathryn had impatiently counted the years, waiting until she could leap into the modern world of the twenty-fourth century, which her friends took for granted. Now she was being sent on an elaborate camping trip. Somehow it didn't seem fair, but she couldn't refuse the assignment. It was her only hope of proving to Commander Brannon that she belonged at Starfleet Academy.

"And here's one of your partners." Captain Holbrook opened a stall door and stepped inside.

Kathryn stared. A huge bird with brown and green body feathers was perched on a wooden bar. As Captain Holbrook put on a leather glove and held out his hand, it screeched and flapped its enormous wings. Green and red feathers rose in warning on its head. The flying predator's beak and talons, evolved for catching and shredding its prey, were sharp and strong.

"Up, Fiona!" The bird obeyed the captain's command and hopped onto the glove. "This is a Baneriam hawk. You won't have much time to learn the voice and hand signals that control her, but I'm sure you'll manage."

"Yes, sir." Kathryn winced at the nervous tremor in her voice, but Captain Holbrook didn't seem to notice. She didn't know anything about birds! And Fiona was eyeing her as if she were today's special on the lunch menu. *What,* Kathryn wondered in a near-panic, *does he expect me to ride?*

"You'll be riding Courtney's Pride," Captain Holbrook said. "Cadet Castille chose him and the horse has already had a week to get used to the other animals."

Kathryn felt only slightly relieved as the captain nodded at the stall across the aisle from the hawk. The large bay thoroughbred snorted, then resumed pacing in small circles.

"We'll work with Fiona on the ground for a while before you bring Pride out." The captain left the stall with the hawk and headed out the back door.

Kathryn paused as Endar, the hook spider, and the *t'stayan* walked by and out into a fenced paddock.

Stepping to the door, she sagged against the doorjamb and sighed.

The young Betazoid, Jon, was sitting on the ground between the serpent's front legs, petting a rock. The Vulcan girl was mounted and walking the *zabathu* around the enclosure with the *sehlat* trotting at its heels. Thorn stood off to one side, holding the *sark*'s reins in one hand, the *targ*'s leash in another, and glaring at everyone. As Endar walked toward the center of the arena, the *t'stayan* suddenly emitted a high-pitched, earsplitting shriek.

The hook spider leaped onto Endar's head and started spitting. The *zabathu* reared, almost unseating T'Lor, the Vulcan girl. The *sehlat* whirled and roared. The serpent squawked and squealed in three-part harmony and sat back on its monstrous tail. Jon's rock sprouted wings and took flight. Fiona, the hawk, launched herself into the air to chase the flying stone. The *targ* and the *sark* bolted, dragging a sputtering Thorn across the paddock through the dirt.

Captain Holbrook whistled for the hawk and shook his head as the bird circled back.

Kathryn watched in stunned dismay. Her future as a cadet was uncertain, but one thing she knew for sure. She had enrolled in Starfleet Academy—not the circus!

Chapter

4

Kathryn led Pride out into the sunshine with a distinct sense of walking toward certain doom. The spirited horse had fidgeted constantly while she groomed and saddled him, and he broke out in a nervous sweat the instant he saw the other animals. Everyone else had settled down.

The alien riders were all walking their mounts around the paddock—Endar with his spider clutched around his neck, Jon with his bag of flying rocks slung over his shoulder, and Thorn and T'Lor with the *targ* and the *sehlat* trotting beside them. They stopped and turned when Captain Holbrook spotted Kathryn and waved.

All eyes were on her again, Kathryn realized uneasily. She had been the center of attention when Captain Holbrook had taken her into the adjoining field to learn the hawk's basic commands. Although Kathryn had no experience with large birds, Fiona was well trained and cooperative. Kathryn didn't have the same confidence in the horse.

Ignoring the mounting block by the door, she lowered the stirrup on the English saddle. She wouldn't always have something to stand on when they got to Diehr IV. She had to be able to mount from the ground. But the horse stood over sixteen hands high, not quite five and a half feet to the withers. Ordinarily, this wouldn't be a problem, but Pride refused to stand still. Kathryn's cheeks flamed red as he sidestepped, making her hop awkwardly for several seconds before she could swing herself into the saddle. Keeping a firm grip on the reins, she slipped her right foot into the right stirrup and reached for the left stirrup leather to adjust it back to the correct length.

With Fiona perched on his gloved arm, Captain Holbrook walked out the gate toward her.

The hawk ruffled its feathers.

And Pride bolted.

Gripping the saddle with her legs, Kathryn ignored the loose stirrup bumping against her boot and fought the horse for control. She was halfway across the field before she managed to stop, turn, and start back to the paddock.

"What else can you expect from a girl?" Endar asked Thorn. The Klingon laughed.

T'Lor glanced at them, but her face was a mask of unemotional calm.

"She didn't fall off!" Jon rose to Kathryn's defense, but he looked as worried as the captain.

Although their animals had not been perfect models of behavior, either, Kathryn could hardly blame them. She must have looked like a total fool. None of them had made a friendly overture since Captain Holbrook had introduced her. Maybe they had all made friends with Cadet Castille and resented her for taking his place.

"Having a few problems, Kathryn?" Captain Holbrook asked with a sigh of exasperation.

"Yes, sir." Kathryn hesitated, hoping he wouldn't interpret the request she was about to make as an excuse. She didn't make excuses for herself, but there was a problem and it had a simple solution. "I want another horse. Pride is totally unsuitable for this mission."

A slow smile brightened Captain Holbrook's face as he nodded. It was not the reaction Kathryn expected.

"Excellent decision, Kathryn. I tried to convince Mr. Castille to change mounts, but he was too attached to Pride. I thought he might calm down with a different rider, but he's just too high-strung. Better to introduce a new horse now, while we still have a week to train."

"Thank you, sir." Dismounting, Kathryn kept the reins looped over Pride's neck and gripped them under his chin. That way, if he spooked and ran again, he wouldn't trip on or break the dangling reins.

"Just have Lieutenant Commander Ralston show you what he's got and pick one out."

"Giving up already, Cadet?" Thorn hooted as Kathryn headed toward the main barn.

"That's enough, Thorn," Captain Holbrook commanded firmly. "Kathryn will be right back."

Chin up and shoulders squared, Kathryn kept walking. She wasn't going to let the team's remarks get to her, but she couldn't avoid her father's voice echoing in her brain.

You never get a second chance to make a first impression, Kathryn.

She had blown her one and only chance to make a good *first* impression, but maybe she could make up the lost ground on the second.

However, as Ted Ralston led Kathryn through the stable, she began to have her doubts. The Academy owned a string of lesson horses that were calm, but they were either too old or too set in their ways. Each had a particular bad habit or trick they could get away with when carrying inexperienced riders. Although time and a dedicated trainer could correct such habits, Kathryn didn't have the time.

There were also several show horses, all of them thoroughbreds like Pride and Shawnee and all of them too high-spirited to be safe in unknown, potentially hazardous conditions. Kathryn was headed for a wilderness planet with a group of ill-mannered, alien animals and their hostile handlers. She needed a calm, sturdy, dependable horse.

And Starfleet doesn't seem to have one, Kathryn

thought despondently as they reached the end of the line. Then she spotted a short-coupled buckskin with a black mane and tail in a pasture behind the barn.

"What about that one?"

"Tango?" Lieutenant Commander Ralston threw up his hands. "I forgot about him, but he's perfect!"

"How come he's out to pasture?" Kathryn asked as Ralston grabbed a halter and headed across the yard.

"Most of the cadets prefer these snazzy thoroughbreds." The lieutenant commander winked. "A dumpy-looking quarter horse like Tango just can't compete when it comes to flash. No sense making him stand in a stall all day waiting for a rider that never comes."

"Quarter horse, huh?" Kathryn felt like she had hit the jackpot. Bred to run a fast quarter-mile when cleared land was scarce during American colonial times, the hardy, even-tempered, quick-turning quarter horse had moved on to herd cattle in the American West. It seemed fitting to take a quarter horse to the stars, too.

Kathryn grinned as Ralston whistled and Tango lifted his head. The little horse was waiting at the gate when they got there.

When Kathryn rode Tango back to the paddock, Captain Holbrook gave her a thumbs-up, but she already knew she had made a wise choice. With the Western tack, she could mount in a second and carry more gear and supplies. The horse's shorter stride was easy to sit and she'd be able to ride for hours without wearing herself out.

"He's kind of short, isn't he?" Thorn sneered as Kathryn rode by.

"Yes, he is."

"He can't be very fast," Endar scoffed.

Annoyed, Kathryn just shrugged as she passed Jon's serpent and stopped. Lifting the reins and pulling slightly to the left, she touched Tango in the right side with her heel. He pivoted on his hindquarters to end up facing the same direction as everyone else. With a gentle tug, she backed him into line beside the lizard.

"He's quite obedient," T'Lor said.

"And he's not afraid of Rayonica, either!" Jon beamed at Kathryn, then cocked his head a moment. "That other horse made Rayonica really nervous. This one hardly upsets her at all."

Kathryn blinked, then remembered that the Betazoid boy could read the serpent's thoughts.

"Okay, people!" Captain Holbrook called for everyone's attention. "We'll be staying in the ring today so Kathryn and Tango can get used to working with Fiona."

Kathryn tensed as she slipped the leather glove over her left hand and arm and walked Tango into the center of the paddock. Captain Holbrook spent several minutes moving around the horse with the bird and transferring Fiona from his arm to Kathryn's. Tango's ears flicked nervously at first, but he didn't go berserk. Then the captain asked her to back the horse off a few feet.

Desperately hoping Tango wouldn't buck, shy, or

bolt, Kathryn lifted her arm and called sharply, "Fiona! Here!"

Tango started to back up as the bird flew toward them. Kathryn squeezed her legs to stop him and flinched slightly as the bird landed and gripped the leather with her talons. Kathryn held her there a minute, then gave the command to fly. The great hawk circled overhead until Captain Holbrook told her to call it back. Kathryn's heart fluttered with excitement and she felt a deep sense of satisfaction when Fiona responded and came right to her.

"Now try walking Tango around the ring."

Urging the horse into a walk, Kathryn felt the tension ease from her muscles and his. Fiona raised her tucked wings to balance herself on Kathryn's arm, but within a few minutes the bird adjusted to the ambling rhythm of Tango's gait and Kathryn began to feel comfortable.

As the hours passed and horse, hawk, and human became a functional unit, Kathryn found that she was actually enjoying herself. If the team could just resolve some of their differences, the mission might even be fun!

The sun was plunging toward the horizon when Kathryn put Tango in Pride's old stall. She latched the door and rubbed her shoulder with a heavy sigh.

"You're not used to riding all day, are you?" T'Lor closed her grooming box, then unclipped the *zabathu* from the cross-ties and led the animal into its stall. "There you go, Shammi."

"No, I'm not," Kathryn admitted with a wince. As

much as she had wanted to escape her traditional family home, she wished she could soak in a bathtub tonight. A sonic shower might not have the same soothing effect on sore, stiff muscles, and she'd pay for that tomorrow. Even so, she felt oddly energized after the long and grueling workout.

"A hot bath and some Vulcan liniment will help."

"A bath?" Kathryn started, then smiled. "I thought only Jon could read minds."

"Actually, Jon Brezi cannot read our thoughts. He can only sense animal minds. He's very sensitive about the deficiency."

"Deficiency?" Kathryn frowned. "I think being able to communicate with animals, to *know* what they're thinking and feeling, is a wonderful talent."

"You're not a Betazoid. Come, Choka." The large *sehlat* yawned, then dutifully jumped up and followed T'Lor down the aisle. "You, too, Kathryn. We'll stop by your dorm to get your things."

"My things?" Kathryn checked Fiona to make sure the Baneriam hawk was secure for the night, then limped after the Vulcan girl.

"We'll be rooming together in a house near here until we leave for Diehr Four. There's a bathtub."

"Excellent." However, Kathryn's anticipation of a long soak in hot water was pushed to the back of her mind when she emerged into the courtyard.

Jon was desperately trying to reach the leather bag full of flying rocks that Thorn was holding just beyond his grasp. T'Lor watched in remote, curious silence. Endar sat on a bench with his eyes closed and the black, fuzzy Fooz curled up in his lap. The Talarian wasn't the least bit concerned about the Klingon's cruel teasing.

"Give them back to me, Thorn!"

"But I'm curious, Jon. Will they break if I drop them?" Thorn let go of the bag, then caught it again with lightning-quick reflexes. He laughed when Jon cringed.

"It is more likely they will attack," T'Lor said evenly. "I've heard the sandbats from Manark Four can be rather vicious when provoked."

"And in this case," Kathryn said icily, "an attack would be justified."

"This is only a contest of wills. A game to make Jon strong." Scowling, Thorn tossed the bag back to the boy.

Jon fumbled the leather pouch as it hit him in the chest, but he saved it from falling. He immediately sank to his knees and gently placed the bag on the ground. The sides bulged as the agitated sandbats shifted around inside. Jon closed his eyes and placed his hands on the bag, not daring to open it in case one of his notoriously dangerous pets tried to escape to get revenge.

"Are they all right?" Kathryn asked.

Jon nodded, picked up the bag, and ran back to the barn.

"Women," Endar muttered in disgust and looked at Kathryn narrowly. "Jon must fight his own battles and learn to defend himself if he expects to be a warrior. On *my* world, he would be humiliated if a female interfered."

"We're not *on* your world, Endar," Kathryn

snapped. It was the first time the Talarian had spoken directly to her or T'Lor all day.

Kathryn's father and mother had discussed life on the Talarian homeworld during a period of intense hostilities a few years ago. The planet was ruled by a patriarchal society, but Kathryn hadn't believed women were excluded from everything except raising children and taking care of their homes. It didn't make sense to waste half the potential of a world's population. However, a few hours of dealing with Endar's rigid refusal to address her and T'Lor, let alone accept them as serious members of the team, had changed that misconception. And, Kathryn thought coldly, a perception adjustment was in order for the Talarian, too. Human and Vulcan females were *not* the inconvenient, nonessential, weak creatures he believed them to be.

"How does anyone on your world survive to become an adult if the older and stronger kids are allowed to prey on younger and smaller children?" Kathryn deliberately glared at the boy. Direct confrontation might get him to respond.

"Only the strong survive, but that's something a *girl* couldn't possibly understand."

"Jon is not a Talarian and I don't believe he has any desire to be a warrior," T'Lor said. "Therefore, this discussion is irrelevant."

"See? Trying to explain anything to a woman is a waste of time." Cradling the spider, Endar rose and walked away without another word.

Kathryn sighed. T'Lor was correct in her logic, but

she assumed that all societies were logical, too. A lot of them weren't. Endar respected strength and aggression, not reason. At least he had answered Kathryn's question.

"I do not understand how your mighty Federation survives when it is *infected* with so much weakness." Snarling, Thorn called his *targ* and stomped off after Endar.

"Do you still want that bath, Kathryn?" T'Lor asked.

"Yes, but maybe we should make sure Jon is okay first."

"He's with the serpent." T'Lor spoke matter-of-factly, as though Kathryn's suggestion were completely irrational. "No one dares bother him in Rayonica's stall. That's why he goes there."

"That's not what I meant. I—" Kathryn choked back the rest of her words. True to Vulcan tradition, T'Lor had suppressed her emotions so thoroughly, she was not aware of the emotional needs of others. For all Kathryn knew, Jon *had* fled to Rayonica because he wanted to be left alone.

As Kathryn followed T'Lor down the drive, she was suddenly overwhelmed with weariness. Five minutes of trying to cope with so many diverse and incompatible alien personalities was infinitely more tiring than spending ten hours in the saddle making friends with a bird.

And, she realized grimly, it was obvious that they felt the same way about her.

Chapter

5

A rush of anxious anticipation coursed through Kathryn as Captain Holbrook walked onto the cargo loading dock. She chirped at Fiona in her travel cage and scratched Tango's neck. The gesture, she realized, steadied her nerves. The horse was more tranquil than any of them.

"This is it, people." Captain Holbrook rubbed his hands together and smiled. "We've got some time before we begin transporting to the science vessel *U.S.S. McMurray,* so we might as well put it to good use."

Kathryn bit her lower lip to keep from smiling and sternly reminded herself *why* they were going to Diehr IV. The mission was a serious test of Captain Holbrook's proposal to use animals in Starfleet. If the team failed to complete the exercise successfully, the captain's program would not get funding. And his reputation and credibility might be irrevocably damaged.

Still, Kathryn mused, she was about to transport to an Oberth-class starship for a two-day journey to an alien planet on a real mission. She couldn't help it. She was thrilled. She smiled.

"Diehr Four is very much like Earth prior to its technological development," Captain Holbrook continued. "The target area is a forested mountain region with plenty of running water and forage for the animals."

"A picnic!" Thorn spat out the English word.

Kathryn shook her head. During the past week, she had learned something about her companions. Except for Jon, everyone attended the major educational institution on his or her homeworld.

Thorn's father, a member of the Klingon High Council, had ordered his oldest son to participate in the mission as a means of advancing cooperation and understanding between the Federation and the Klingon Empire. Thorn had agreed under protest. He did not believe his warrior race could possibly benefit from an alliance with the "weak" peoples of the Federation. His attitude might have disastrous consequences for the Federation in the future. Thorn came from a powerful family and would probably sit on the Klingon High Council himself one day.

Captain Holbrook ignored Thorn's remark. "Keep in mind that even though the plants on Diehr Four are not poisonous to you or the animals, they will not provide adequate nutrition. You must remember to feed your animals and yourselves the food supplements you'll be carrying with you."

"We would not have food supplements if we crash-landed on an alien world," Endar said.

"That is true, Endar," the captain replied patiently. "But this is not a survival exercise. Your mission is to extract a surveillance probe with a malfunctioning camouflage field before the region's native tribe finds it or spots you."

Kathryn studied the Talarian's brooding face. Holbrook had taken advantage of an uneasy truce to contact the Talarian government regarding the study. The captain had hopes of stabilizing relations between the Federation and Endar's homeworld by exposing the Talarian teenager to young people from other worlds. Holbrook believed that working closely with kids from different cultures would show Endar how much the various races had in common. So far, Kathryn reflected, Endar had made no effort to acquaint himself with anyone except Thorn. He had volunteered for the mission because he wanted to gather intelligence for the Talarians to use *against* the Federation in future conflicts.

"I thought this planet didn't have any people," Jon said, frowning.

Captain Holbrook chuckled. "It doesn't. We're going to *pretend* there's a primitive race on the planet as part of the mission parameters."

"Oh." Jon nodded and lowered his gaze.

Kathryn wished she could help the Betazoid boy

resolve his troubles, but Jon was still a puzzle. One moment he was outgoing and happy, and then suddenly he would withdraw. Captain Holbrook had told her that no one knew if Jon's telepathic abilities were emerging later than normal for his race or if they were permanently impaired. Kathryn had developed a huge amount of respect for Jon. Although he felt handicapped by his "deficiency," he had not let it stop him from using the talent he had. At eleven, he was several years younger than everyone else. He had been asked to join the study because no one else could control the potentially useful, but ordinarily uncontrollable, Sehgal serpent and Manark IV sandbats.

"You'll be beamed in through a narrow window in a *pretend* ionized atmosphere, too," Captain Holbrook added.

"What is the point of creating obstacles that do not exist?" T'Lor asked.

Kathryn suppressed a grin. The Vulcan was genuinely bewildered by the concept of "make-believe." T'Lor was equally mystified by the tendency of other races to soften truth. Kathryn herself had been forced to hide her true feelings when T'Lor announced that she intended to pursue a diplomatic career. Ambassador Sarek was T'Lor's hero, or at least the Vulcan equivalent of one. However, whether Sarek had learned his diplomatic skills from being married to a human and raising his half-human son, Spock, or from experience, he knew it was sometimes necessary to curb blunt and brutal truth to keep opposing governments negotiating. Nor was it productive to attack an individual's self-esteem or insult his culture. Kathryn liked T'Lor in spite of her unyielding dedication to total honesty without regard to the consequences. She had tried to explain the difference between an outright lie and evading or shading destructive truth, but T'Lor just didn't get it. With luck, Kathryn thought, the fate of the Federation would never depend on T'Lor's diplomatic abilities!

Captain Holbrook deftly fielded T'Lor's question without making her feel stupid for asking it. Although, Kathryn realized, his consideration for her feelings was probably lost on the Vulcan.

"The mission would not be a thorough test of using animals in nontechnological situations if there weren't any obstacles to overcome or specific criteria to satisfy. *But,*" the captain emphasized, "since Starfleet does not send students on dangerous missions, it's necessary to establish fabricated conditions instead. Like a simulation."

T'Lor nodded thoughtfully. "Yes, that is logical."

The transporter chief entered and the discussion ended. Captain Holbrook directed Kathryn and her animals to beam up first. Nothing seemed to upset the quarter horse, and Holbrook was counting on Tango's calm nature to soothe his alien companions when they arrived in the ship's cargo bay. Stalls and supplies were already set up and waiting.

As Kathryn led Tango up the ramp to the transporter pad, she was struck by an unexpected and powerful realization. She had worked her whole life to get accepted into Starfleet Academy and she had succeeded. But then, on the eve of leaving for school, she had discovered that the prospect of a Starfleet career no longer excited her. Since she had arrived on campus, that lack of desire had nagged at her even though she had subconsciously ignored it. It had shadowed her through classes and simulations and all the way into Commander Brannon's office. She hadn't been sure Starfleet was what she wanted or where she belonged.

Now, as Kathryn waited to beam up to the science ship with a horse and a hawk, she suddenly knew. Starfleet was the only place in the universe Kathryn Janeway wanted to be.

But Commander Brannon still had to be convinced.

And this mission was her best chance, maybe even her last chance, to prove she belonged at Starfleet Academy.

The transporter chief's hand paused over the controls as a clattering of heavy feet drew everyone's attention.

Hov nej, whose name translated as Star Seeker, apparently wanted to go back to the barn. Thorn was struggling to keep the armor-plated, organic tank from leaving.

"Mev!" The Klingon commanded the *sark* to stop and pushed against the animal's chest. Neither action had any effect until Jup jumped in front of Hov nej and squealed.

The *targ* stopped the *sark*.

And upset most of the other animals.

Kathryn tightened her grip on Tango's lead shank

when his head snapped up, but he didn't jump or bolt. Fiona shrieked from the cage sitting on the adjacent transporter disk, and Kathryn cooed to quiet her.

The *sehlat*, Choka, sprang protectively in front of T'Lor and roared. Shammi, the Vulcan's white *zabathu*, kicked, toppling a stack of cargo canisters. Perched on Endar's head, Fooz began spitting. The silver-haired *t'stayan* almost gored Rayonica with his ribbed horn. Jon screamed as the dinosaur lunged backward. Her right head flicked a lightning-fast tongue toward the tasty-looking spider.

Leaping out of range, Endar yanked Ginjar away from the serpent and set the hook spider on the *t'stayan*'s back. Without a word of warning, he stormed toward Thorn and slammed his fist into the Klingon's jaw. Thorn staggered in surprise, then rammed Endar in the stomach with his head, sending both of them sprawling on the floor.

Captain Holbrook waved to the transporter chief as he hurried across the floor to stop the brawl.

As the warm tingle of molecular dematerialization washed through Kathryn, her mind focused on a single thought. Staying in the Academy and completing Holbrook's study mission were not her biggest problems.

The team would be lucky to survive one another.

Chapter

6

To Kathryn's surprise, the journey to Diehr IV aboard the *U.S.S. McMurray* passed without another disruptive incident between team members.

Although Endar refused to apologize for attacking Thorn on the cargo loading dock, the Klingon did not hold a grudge. Both boys had been struggling to keep their aggressive natures under control during training at the Academy for the mission. The fight had taken the edge off the explosive pressures building within them. On the ship they had spent their free time playing Parrises Squares with the *McMurray* crew. Everyone was relieved that the young warriors had found an acceptable outlet for their violent energies. Kathryn hoped that the trek through the mountains of Diehr

IV would be so physically exhausting that Endar and Thorn would be too tired to fight.

T'Lor had taken every opportunity to observe and talk with crew members from several different species. Her curiosity was welcome even though her blunt questions and remarks sometimes left her study subjects stunned and speechless. However, the Vulcan's total lack of tact was balanced by a guileless innocence and genuine interest that the seasoned ship's personnel found oddly charming. Still, hoping to avert an intergalactic incident of cataclysmic proportions in the near or distant future, Kathryn continued to coach T'Lor in the art of diplomacy. Most of the time she felt like she was talking to the proverbial brick wall.

Jon kept to himself, turning to Rayonica and the sandbats for company when the team wasn't busy with preparations.

When they assembled in the *McMurray*'s cargo bay to be transported to the surface of Diehr IV, Kathryn was brimming with confidence. Everyone worked together, checking gear and loading supply packs onto their animals. For the first time since joining the expedition, she actually felt like they could pull it off.

Captain Holbrook looked pleased and relieved as he gave them their final instructions. "The surveillance probe is located near the native tribe's ceremonial site. It's marked on your maps. You must remove the probe and leave the area before the tribe arrives to conduct a seasonal ritual at dawn the day after tomorrow. It should take you roughly a day and a half to reach the site."

"The probe is really there, but the native people aren't, right?" Jon asked.

The captain nodded. "Once you've got the probe, you'll have the rest of tomorrow and the next day to reach the beam-out site. Transport off Diehr Four is scheduled for sundown. If you're late, you'll miss the window."

"In the ionized atmosphere that really isn't ionized," Thorn muttered.

"You won't be stranded on the planet if you're late, Thorn." Holbrook eyed the Klingon narrowly. "But if all the conditions we've established for the mission aren't satisfied, you'll fail."

Thorn puffed out his chest. "Klingons do not fail."

"I hope not." Holbrook paused. "One more thing. Although we won't be in direct communication with you, we *will* be monitoring your progress and activities through your locator badges. If a real danger should arise, you'll be beamed out immediately."

Endar and Thorn glanced at each other and rolled their eyes. For once, Kathryn agreed with them. If Holbrook transported the team off the planet at the first sign of trouble, they wouldn't have a fair chance to test themselves or his theories. Like Thorn, Kathryn did not want to fail.

"See you in three days. Good luck." Holbrook stepped back and nodded to Kathryn. Since Tango's quiet presence had a calming effect on the other animals, she had been chosen to go first again.

With Fiona perched on her leather-gloved hand, Kathryn led the horse onto the transporter pad and rode a phased matter stream through the vacuum of space to an alien wilderness world. She materialized in a clearing surrounded by tall, lush trees with broad, emerald green leaves. The pungent musk of decaying vegetation hung in the cool air, teasing her nostrils. She heard the splash of water cascading over rocks in a stream nearby. Lifting his head, Tango snorted and stamped his foot. The hawk flapped her wings, anxious to fly after two days of confinement.

"Soon, Fiona," Kathryn murmured as Thorn appeared.

Hov nej and Jup both shook themselves and grunted. The Klingon, *sark,* and *targ* all tilted their heads back and tested the alien scents wafting from the forest. Thorn drew in a deep breath and nodded approval.

"It's invigorating, isn't it?" Kathryn sensed that the Klingon was as comfortable in the primal forests as he was in a twenty-fourth-century starship. Unlike humans', the Klingon race's primitive instincts had not become dulled as they adapted to controlled environments and technology. She found that strangely comforting.

"Yes! It makes the longing to hunt run hot in the blood!" A rare smile curled the corner of Thorn's mouth as he pulled a map out of his saddlebag.

Jon blinked as the transporter beam deposited him and Rayonica on firm ground. The dinosaur's heads adjusted themselves to scan in all directions. The boy's eyes widened as he looked around, then caught Kathryn's gaze. "This *is* a wild place, isn't it?"

Kathryn smiled to reassure him. "Nothing you can't handle, Jon. I think Rayonica likes it."

The serpent sniffed the rich soil with her center head, froze, then snatched a burrowing beetle into her mouth with her tongue. The other two heads calmly continued to scan the strange surroundings. Jon laughed and relaxed.

Even Endar looked pleased with the wild beauty of Diehr IV. The *t'stayan* and the hook spider remained calm in the unfamiliar environment, and Kathryn wondered if the Talarian homeworld was similar. She would have asked, but she didn't want Endar to accuse her of fishing for sensitive information again. Since he was using the mission to spy on the Federation, he assumed the Federation members of the team were gathering intelligence on his world, too.

T'Lor only glanced around with mild curiosity. Choka, the *sehlat,* immediately began to walk the perimeter of the clearing, checking for unseen dangers. The camel-like Shammi snapped her head up and tensed. The *zabathu*'s ears flicked toward the sound of the stream, and a nervous twitch rippled down her skin.

"Easy, Shammi." T'Lor soothed the *zabathu.* "She's from a desert planet. Maybe running water upsets her."

"She'll have to get used to it," Thorn growled. He tapped the map he had unfolded and placed on a large rock. "The shortest route to the ceremonial cliff follows the river through a canyon to the west."

T'Lor frowned.

"Rayonica likes water," Jon said.

Kathryn dropped Tango's reins and went to peer over Thorn's shoulder. The horse had been trained to ground-tie and would not move until she told him to. Although they had been thoroughly briefed about the terrain, the weather, and the wildlife on the planet, the route had not been decided prior to landing as part of the exercise.

"If we go that way, Thorn, we'll have to climb the steep side of the mountain to reach the probe." Kathryn stabbed her finger at the elevation on the map. She did not want to point out that the Andorian *zaba-thu* might not be willing or able to navigate a river route.

"No problem." Endar patted the six-legged *t'stay-an*'s neck. "Ginjar can climb anything."

"But the other animals can't," Kathryn countered. "We have to choose a path that's passable for everyone. One that exposes us to the least amount of danger."

"You don't have to worry, human," Thorn rumbled. "If you are in danger, Captain Holbrook will beam you out before you get hurt."

"I have no intention of being beamed out until the mission is completed, Thorn." Kathryn stiffened. "And I don't think you understand what Captain Holbrook meant."

"What did he mean?" Endar asked suspiciously.

"If we run into trouble, we'll *all* be transported back to the ship. This isn't a contest. It's a mission. Either the *whole* team makes it—or none of us do."

Thorn scowled. "If this were a Klingon mission, the *only* objective would be getting the probe out. It would not matter how many were lost along the way as long as one succeeded in the end."

"This is not a Klingon mission." T'Lor eyed Thorn levelly and pressed closer to the *zabathu*. "No one is expendable."

Although she wouldn't say so, the Vulcan did not want any harm to come to Shammi, Kathryn realized. If water made the Andorian animal nervous, she might panic, bolt, and injure herself on the rocks. The team had to take *all* the animals' needs into consideration.

"We should go northwest," Kathryn suggested. "We'll gain altitude gradually and all the animals can handle the terrain."

Endar scanned the map. "That route is longer. It'll add hours to the trip."

"Will we get to the probe site on time?" Jon asked hesitantly.

"It'll be tight," Kathryn admitted, "but we can make it."

"We only have three days to secure the probe and reach the beam-out point," Thorn insisted. "Better to save as much time as we can."

"Saving time won't mean anything if we don't get there at all." Kathryn matched the Klingon's stubborn gaze.

"A logical and accurate conclusion, Thorn," T'Lor said.

Kathryn's earlier expectations about successfully

completing the mission began to unravel. They hadn't even left the landing site and already they were hopelessly at odds. If they couldn't agree on a route, they wouldn't be able to agree on a lot of things. They'd waste more time arguing than they would taking the longer, but safer, trail.

"Who put you in command?" Endar glared at Kathryn.

Kathryn started. Why hadn't Captain Holbrook appointed someone as team leader? It was a good question, and she could reach only one conclusion. Klingons and Talarians had been sworn enemies of the Federation for a long time. A fragile, and perhaps temporary, peace did not automatically dissolve the bad feelings that had existed between them. Maybe this wasn't just a study of how animals might be used in nontech conditions. Maybe *their* ability to cooperate was being tested, too. Captain Holbrook hadn't told them because it wouldn't be a true test if they knew.

But it's a test we seemed doomed to fail, Kathryn thought. She immediately rejected that possibility.

They were five distinctly different races with ten alien animals—all with their individual abilities and limitations and all operating on their own agendas. But if they could learn to work together, to use one another's strengths to offset everyone's weaknesses, they could accomplish everything they had been sent to do!

"Someone has to make a decision," T'Lor said.

"Agreed." Thorn stared at the Vulcan. "We'll take the river route."

Jon raised his hand and spoke cautiously. "I think we should go the way Kathryn said."

"I do *not* take orders from a woman!" Endar's eyes flashed.

Turn this squabbling group into a team? Kathryn's confidence bottomed out as they voted three to two to take the safer northwest route. *Hopeless.*

But it was a challenge she couldn't refuse.

Chapter

7

Kathryn shifted in the saddle, working out the kinks in her muscles. Except for a brief stop to rest and water the animals, they had been moving steadily for almost ten hours. Even after a week of hard training at the Academy stables, her body was beginning to protest. Ahead of her, Kathryn noticed that Jon was slumping with weariness, too.

Not surprising, Kathryn thought as she brushed a wisp of hair off her forehead. Although the ascent through the mountain forest was gradual, they had been climbing upward constantly. There was no trail to follow, and the rocks and undergrowth made the going difficult. At least the animals had settled down.

Kathryn had suggested that the Klingon lead to

soothe his wounded pride when the team voted to take her route instead of his. That diplomatic decision had turned out to have several advantages. The heavy *sark* moved at a pace the other animals could easily match, and nothing stood in its way. Hov nej barged through brush, piles of branches, and tangles of vines like a bulldozer, clearing a path for the smaller, lighter animals.

Jup, whose name meant "friend" in Klingon, would not stray far from Thorn. However, having the *targ* scout the area ahead, routing any unsuspecting alien animals that lurked in the woods, had also been beneficial. Although the *targ*'s path meandered slightly, he led Thorn around impassable obstacles, saving them time and trouble.

T'Lor's *sehlat,* Choka, roamed the surrounding woods, alert and ready to defend them from any hidden dangers. Kathryn was impressed with how fast and silently the large, bearlike creature could move through the dense forest.

Still, it had taken a few hours of trial and error before they finally agreed on everyone else's place in line.

Neither Ginjar nor Fooz liked to be near the Sehgal serpent. According to Jon, the long-haired *t'stayan* was repulsed by the dinosaur's smell and the hook spider did not want to risk being eaten. Endar was not happy that Jon could read his animals' minds, but he had to concede that the information was valuable. Rayonica was not overly fond of the Klingon *sark*. T'Lor's *zabathu* tolerated the saurian, but walked at a slightly faster pace and kept bumping her nose on Rayonica's tail if she followed Jon.

After shifting positions several times, they found an order that worked. Thorn led, followed by T'Lor, then Jon on the serpent. Tango, who didn't mind Rayonica, provided a buffer zone between the lizard and the *t'stayan.*

Endar had objected to being last until Thorn pointed out that the front and rear positions were both open to attack. As warriors, they were obligated to ride point and rear to defend the rest of the group.

Fooz clung to Endar's head, basking in the sun, and Jon's sandbats remained quiet in their bag. The hawk had spent most of the day soaring on the light winds. Like Choka and Jup, Fiona was on guard and ready to screech an alarm at the first sign of approaching trouble.

"Maybe we should start looking for a campsite?" Kathryn was careful not to make it sound like she was giving an order. As the day had progressed, she had discovered that everyone was open to sensible suggestions—even Thorn and Endar.

At the front of the line, Thorn twisted in his saddle to look back with a shake of his head. "We have to cover at least three more kilometers if we want to arrive at the probe site by midafternoon tomorrow."

Kathryn nodded, accepting the Klingon's decision. Thorn had demonstrated an innate ability to calculate the time needed to go a given distance. His estimates, based on the terrain, the incline, and the animals' speed, had been amazingly accurate, and Kathryn trusted his judgment.

"Another hour. Then we'll look for a place." Turning forward again, Thorn pushed Hov nej through a thick stand of brush. The massive *sark* trampled the dense vegetation with a satisfied grunt.

"We have another two hours of daylight, Thorn," Endar called out. "We should keep going."

"The animals are tired, Endar." Kathryn looked back at the Talarian riding behind her. "And so are we." She could ride into the night if necessary, but she didn't want to single out Jon as the weak link.

"Speak for yourself, Cadet," Endar sneered. *"I'm* not tired. If we stop before the sun sets, it'll be because you *women* and the boy can't keep up."

Jon straightened in his saddle. "I can go as long as you can, Endar!"

T'Lor's reaction was more rational. "We'll need light to set up camp and secure the area."

"The Vulcan makes a good point," Thorn said. "I once had a friend who slept on a hill of Klingon fire beetles because he did not check the ground. The humiliation hurt almost as much as the poisonous stings."

"Talarians sleep in trees above such hazards," Endar countered.

"Then you must hope the trees on Diehr Four are not the preferred habitat for snakes." T'Lor glanced back, her expression blank.

Kathryn wasn't sure, but she thought she detected a sparkle of amusement in the Vulcan's eyes. *A hope-*

ful sign for the Vulcan Diplomatic Corps and the galaxy, she thought, hiding a smile.

"Or carnivorous birds." Jon didn't bother to hide the amused smile he beamed at the Talarian.

Kathryn was pleased that the young Betazoid was opening up enough to defend himself. Endar, however, did not appreciate the teasing and had to have the last word.

"That's why Talarians tamed hook spiders. Fooz will protect me from all those dangers."

Sighing, Kathryn settled back in the saddle and let Tango pick his own way. Obviously, the team had not come to terms with all their differences, but they *were* on schedule. That was a major accomplishment, considering. With luck, the rest of the mission would be as uneventful.

But luck changes like the tides on Earth, Kathryn reminded herself as they rode up a rocky incline an hour and a half later. To her left, she saw the orange sun of Diehr IV sinking rapidly toward the horizon, and they had not found a suitable place to camp. The terrain had changed dramatically the minute they had started looking.

"We'll sleep on rocks if we have to," Thorn muttered.

Kathryn peered at her map, trusting Tango to follow the others over the uneven land on his own. "It looks like there's a level spot about a kilometer ahead to the northeast. And there's a small stream not too far from it."

"It'll be dark before we get there." T'Lor stated the obvious.

"I don't think we have any choice, T'Lor. We need water and the only other alternative is to go back."

"Not acceptable. We would lose too much time." Endar gloated over the victory unexpected circumstances had given him. "Because we kept going, we're now two kilometers and almost an hour ahead of where we would have been."

The Talarian was right, Kathryn realized, suddenly remembering Commander Roberts's discussion of the Chance Factor. She had forgotten that lesson, and like everyone else, she had assumed they'd find a good spot to spend the night once they decided to stop. But Diehr IV had thrown them a curve. They had reached a steep barren area on the mountain with few trees, no grass, and no water. Chance had pushed them onward, giving them a head start on tomorrow. But now they were tired, the path was treacherous, and it was getting dark. With no moon to reflect light, it would be *completely* dark. A dozen dangerous surprises could be waiting for them on the trail ahead.

The Chance Factor, as Commander Roberts had said, was a constant. The unpredictable and unexpected was always there, waiting to happen.

But, Kathryn thought as she whistled for Fiona to return from the darkening sky, *it's foolish to think that Chance will always work in our favor.*

It wouldn't.

And it didn't.

The Baneriam hawk came in from the south behind

Kathryn. Flying low, Fiona swooped too close to Endar, startling Fooz. The hissing spider leaped to the attack off Endar's head and barely missed striking the hawk with its poisonous mandibles.

Kathryn gasped as the shrieking bird swept upward and the spider nose-dived into the ground. Tango frantically backed up and broke out in a nervous sweat when Kathryn ordered him to stand still.

Spotting the stunned insect, Jon's serpent whirled. Her three heads moved in perfect unison as six eyes focused on the spider. Endar leaped from Ginjar's back. With six hooves flying, the *t'stayan* bolted, with Choka in determined, howling pursuit. The Talarian boy scooped Fooz up an instant before one of Rayonica's three tongues could snag him for a snack.

Jon's leather bag popped open as he desperately tried to pull the serpent's center head up. Two enraged sandbats took to the alien skies, circled, then buzzed the *zabathu*.

Shammi bucked as the bats zoomed over her head, and kicked Hov nej in the flank. The *sark* squealed and reared, sending Thorn somersaulting backward over her rump to land with a painful jolt on his own hindquarters. Jup trotted over with a worried grunt and began licking the Klingon's reddening face.

Kathryn glanced around in openmouthed astonishment as Fiona landed on her gloved hand, shook her wings, and blinked innocently. Aside from bumps and bruises, no one had been seriously hurt.

The *sehlat* had overtaken the slower *t'stayan* and was herding it back to the group. Endar stroked the purring spider as it climbed onto his shoulder. Jon held a sandbat in each hand, calming them with his thoughts. T'Lor had dismounted and offered her hand to help Thorn. He ignored it, jumped to his feet, and winced as he swung back onto the *sark*'s back.

Reining Hov nej around to face the witnesses, Thorn glared. "I will get revenge on anyone who dares speak of this—ever!"

No one said a word as they mounted up. They had more important things to worry about than Thorn's embarrassment and bruised posterior, Kathryn realized as she urged Tango up the slope.

The sun sank behind a distant mountain, blinding them in a moonless darkness.

The Chance Factor could turn their diminishing hope for success into certain defeat in mere seconds.

It was a lesson she would not forget again.

Chapter

8

Aches and pains were the order of the day. No one complained out loud, but as they continued up the mountain the next morning, Kathryn could tell that everyone was stiff and sore after yesterday's long, hard ride.

The Chance Factor, Kathryn reflected, had been working overtime against them.

They had made camp on the first flat area they had found with trees. However, except for the *t'stayan,* the riding animals couldn't negotiate the steep, rocky banks down to the stream. The team had had to fetch and carry canvas bags of water up to them. Except for Endar, who did not hesitate to boast about Ginjar's nimble climbing ability, they had all sustained minor scratches and bruises scrambling up and down the rocks in the dark.

Then, because they had ridden farther than they intended, Thorn decided they were too close to the pretend native tribe's ceremonial site for a fire. Captain Holbrook had warned them not to do anything that might alert a primitive people to their presence within a specified range. The Klingon wasn't absolutely certain they had crossed that invisible line, but he didn't want to fail one of the mission's objectives by default. The mountain temperature dropped to almost freezing, but they did not build a fire. Fortunately, Starfleet's flash-pack field rations heated automatically when opened and the containers completely biodegraded two hours after being activated.

Using their flashlights, a technological convenience Holbrook had allowed for safety reasons, they had checked the ground for wildlife and rocks, but it was impossible to clear away all the debris. Their bedrolls had not provided enough cushioning between them and the ground, which was cold, hard, and covered with small stones.

The hot meal had been the only high point of the long, dark night. Sighing, Kathryn waved a bright blue butterfly with a six-inch wingspan away from Tango's ears. Even the mild-mannered quarter horse would tolerate only so much. Still, although she had awakened feeling like she had slept in a freezer on a bed of jagged Myrmidon crystals, she was not as miserable as Endar.

The Talarian had stubbornly perched in the forked

trunk of a sturdy tree to sleep. He had not encountered any alien snakes or predatory birds, but he was apparently allergic to something in the bark. He woke up to find his face and hands covered with hives.

Worried in spite of Endar's condescending hostility toward her, Kathryn glanced back as Thorn's trail curved around a large rock outcropping. The ointment T'Lor had in her Vulcan medical kit seemed to be working. The red welts on the Talarian's face were fading. *Hopefully, the itching will stop soon, too,* she thought. Endar was difficult to get along with under the best of circumstances. Embarrassed and covered with itchy, red bumps, he was impossible.

"What are you looking at, Cadet?" Endar snapped.

"Do you want some more of T'Lor's medicine?" Kathryn asked evenly.

"No. Mind your own business."

Shrugging, Kathryn turned her attention back to the terrain. They had entered another section of forest. The trees were taller and there was less underbrush than they had found at the lower elevations. Still, the gradual but constant upward slope slowed their pace. Thorn kept glancing at the time and the map and frowning. Even though their campsite had been uncomfortable, it was probably a stroke of luck that they had covered the extra distance yesterday. They were losing ground today.

"There it is!" Thorn pointed as he steered Hov nej into a small clearing.

Kathryn reined Tango in to stand beside Rayonica as everyone paused to look. She didn't know whether the animals had finally gotten used to one another or if they were just too tired to waste energy throwing tantrums, but they all stayed quiet.

High on the mountain in the distance, the ceremonial ledge jutted out from a sheer cliff. The surveillance probe was hidden in a cleft cut into the face of the rock. Kathryn guessed the site was about five kilometers away—as the Baneriam hawk flies. Getting to it was not going to be a straight shot for the riding animals, she realized as Endar called their attention to the downward slope of the terrain ahead.

A deep, impassable gorge ran between the mountain they were on and the mountain height that rose before them.

"Which is the shortest way around it?" T'Lor asked.

Thorn shrugged. "I don't know. It's not on the map."

Endar scowled at Kathryn. "It'll be your fault if we can't get past the gorge, Janeway. It was your idea to go this way."

Jon hung his head. He had voted for Kathryn's route along with T'Lor.

"Placing blame won't solve anything," T'Lor said. "We all voted and agreed."

Kathryn was not going to defend a decision that made perfect sense given the available information. "We have to decide what to do now."

"We go east," Thorn said.

"Why?" T'Lor asked.

Thorn set his jaw. "East or west, we've got a fifty-

fifty chance of picking the best route around that ravine."

Not good enough, Kathryn thought as the *sehlat* came bounding out of the trees from the west. Choka ran up to T'Lor, whined excitedly, and ran back into the forest. Several seconds later, the huge, fanged creature returned, sat down, and whined again.

"I think we should follow the *sehlat.*" Kathryn didn't hesitate to make the suggestion. If her hunch was wrong, the time lost would doom the mission. But that was a chance she had to take. Bramble had led her out of too many tight spots in the Indiana woods for her to ignore Choka's obvious signals. The *sehlat* had already found the best route. The team just had to listen.

"Yes." T'Lor nodded. "Choka knows the way."

Thorn looked down at the *targ*. "Which way, Jup?"

The *targ* grunted and wagged its stubby tail, but it didn't move one way or the other.

Endar's eyes flashed defiantly. "We should go east, Thorn. If we let these women and that boy make another decision, we'll never reach the probe."

"That is completely illogical reasoning." T'Lor's voice had a slight edge. "I agree with Kathryn. We should go west after Choka."

Thorn's eyes narrowed. "East."

Jon flinched as everyone turned to stare at him. Once again, the Betazoid had the deciding vote.

"Trust your own instincts, Jon," Kathryn said gently.

Nodding, Jon took a deep breath and closed his

eyes. The serpent's middle neck flexed as Jon loosened his hold on the reins and talked to her with telepathy. A tense moment passed. Three heads turned together as the dinosaur moved out on her own—heading west on the *sehlat*'s trail.

Kathryn reined Tango to follow and released Fiona into the sky. T'Lor fell into place behind the horse. Five minutes later, Thorn and Endar brought up the rear in sullen silence.

Choka was waiting for them where the slope met the sheer drop into the ravine. When they caught up, the *sehlat* led them down a wide, gradually descending ledge to the base of the gorge. There was a secondary split in the rock face on the opposite side. Letting Endar lead on the surefooted *t'stayan,* the team entered the narrow, winding canyon. An hour later, they emerged from the rock walls onto the forested slope of the ceremonial mountain. At most, they had lost half an hour.

Taking their usual places in line, the group moved steadily upward toward the probe without speaking. Kathryn was very much aware that the animals were beginning to function as a better team than their intelligent, but stubborn, handlers.

Still, Kathryn felt a growing respect for her companions. Although T'Lor's diplomatic skills left a lot to be desired, her logical approach had a stabilizing effect. Rather than giving in to their pride and aggressive impulses, Thorn and Endar had held their tempers in check for the good of the mission. And Jon had shown courage by sticking to his convictions in spite of his lack of confidence and feelings of inadequacy.

Even she had gained some valuable insights, Kathryn mused. Everyone on the team, including the animals, had something significant to add to the whole. Although she didn't trust everyone's motives, she had learned to trust their individual talents. Separately, they couldn't do the job. As a unit they could. It would just be a lot easier if they could overcome their differences of opinion and cultivated prejudices.

Seeing Fiona begin a circling descent overhead, Kathryn called the hawk back to rest for a while.

As they neared the clearing by the ceremonial cliff, the forest became more majestic. Almost no underbrush grew beneath the high, thick canopy of needled branches on the giant trees, and very little light filtered through. Dust motes danced in the few rays of sunshine that penetrated the forest gloom. Captain Holbrook had chosen his pretend ritual gathering place well. There was an eerie, almost mystic quality to the shadowed landscape.

"This is it," Thorn announced calmly as he rode the *sark* into a clearing. The ground was carpeted in a spongy moss that muted the sound of hooves.

"Are we on time?" Endar asked as he dismounted and tied Ginjar to a tree.

"Yes, but we do not have time to spare." T'Lor slid off the *zabathu* and stretched. Choka nuzzled her hand for a pat on the head, then ran off to check the woods. Draping the reins over Shammi's neck, the

Vulcan took a handful of nutrition pellets out of her saddlebag and dropped them on the ground.

Kathryn did the same for Tango and sent Fiona skyward to scout the surrounding forest from the air. She felt a distinct sense of satisfied triumph everyone seemed to share. Even though they didn't have any margin for error, they had reached the site on schedule. And they had a fighting chance of reaching the beam-out point on time, too.

Hov nej and Jup lowered themselves to the ground as Thorn walked to the cliff to locate the malfunctioning probe.

Kathryn paused beside the Klingon as he knelt to peer over the edge. She swayed slightly as she looked down. The ledge they were standing on jutted out from the side of the mountain. However, the rock platform sloped inward again under them, giving her a sense of being suspended in midair. The cliff itself was a sheer drop, and the bottom was too far down to be seen. She took a step back.

"Very clever." Thorn actually grinned. "No one could find this probe unless they knew where to look."

Kathryn frowned. The compact surveillance probe was wedged into a cleft where the rock ledge curved under. "But how do we get it out?" She did not add what else she was thinking. *Without falling.*

"Good question," Jon said. "I don't want to climb down over the edge."

"We brought rope." Endar shook his head in disgust. "Now we know why. I'll go."

"That won't be necessary." As T'Lor knelt beside the Klingon, Fiona suddenly screeched overhead.

Kathryn had never heard the bird call exactly that way before. Captain Holbrook had just described it. It was the hawk's shrill warning of danger.

Everyone looked up, including the tethered riding animals they had left at the edge of the clearing. Tango, Shammi, and Ginjar pranced nervously. Fooz folded his legs into the *t'stayan*'s long hair to get a more secure grip. The *sark* grunted as she started to stand up. Rayonica drew back her heads and hissed. The sandbats stirred inside the leather bag hanging from her saddle. The *targ* raised his snout to test scent.

The *sehlat* yelped in pain somewhere in the woods.

Kathryn's heart thudded against her ribs as she turned toward the sound of Choka's cry.

A monstrous catlike animal with greenish brown fur and gleaming fangs burst out of the forest with an enraged roar. It charged toward them with unbelievable speed.

The Chance Factor had finally hit them with a life-and-death crisis. Kathryn dropped to one knee, prepared to spring aside. It was a futile exercise. They were all trapped on a ledge that ended in thin air on three sides.

There was nowhere to run.

Chapter

The next few seconds unfolded in slow motion for Kathryn as the alien cat raced toward the cliff and easy prey. She could imagine only three possible endings to the terrifying situation.

Captain Holbrook would beam them out of danger.

The cat would turn before grabbing one of them to munch for lunch.

Or someone was going to be pushed off the cliff.

Thorn and Endar jumped in front of Kathryn, T'Lor, and Jon, then crouched to repel the cat's attack. Standing on the edge opposite Kathryn, T'Lor wrapped her arm around Jon's shoulder and drew him close. The boy was wide-eyed and frozen with fear.

Kathryn picked up a rock and tensed as she focused

on the cat. The moment it sprang toward Thorn or Endar, she would launch a counterattack. Together, the three of them might be able to fight it off without being ripped to shreds or falling off the cliff. *Why,* she wondered, *isn't Captain Holbrook initiating an emergency beam-out?*

The powerful cat leaped toward Thorn.

Thorn raised his hands to grapple with the animal when it struck.

But the cat never touched the Klingon.

Shrieking in fury, the *targ* charged and rammed into the cat's side just as it left the ground. Jup's forward momentum deflected the cat and sent both of them plunging off the ledge in a tangle of snarling fur and fangs.

"NOOOO!" Thorn sprang to the edge to peer down.

Endar and T'Lor blinked in dazed surprise. Jon pulled away from the Vulcan and knelt beside the Klingon. The Betazoid's face twisted in anguish as he closed his eyes and reached out to the falling *targ.*

Kathryn went to stand behind them, placing a comforting hand on the Klingon's broad shoulder. Losing Jup brought the painful memory of Bramble's death flooding back. She blinked back her tears and silently mourned, not just for the little dog that had shared her growing-up years, but for the devoted *targ.* In a tragic way, Kathryn realized sadly, Jup's sacrifice proved that Captain Holbrook was right about the value of animals in nontechnological circumstances. The *targ* had been as effective as a phaser.

Agonizing seconds passed before Jon glanced at Thorn. A deep sorrow glazed the boy's eyes. "I can't sense his mind anymore, Thorn."

Thorn nodded, his jaw flexing as he struggled to control the pain of his loss. "He's dead."

Jon frowned slightly as he stared into Thorn's eyes. "Yes, but Jup gave his life to save yours because he loved you. He was not afraid. He died instantly, without pain. I felt it."

Kathryn stepped back as Thorn met Jon's gaze and gripped the boy's arms in his massive hands.

"Jup died a warrior's death, Thorn." Endar swallowed hard and his voice trembled.

"Ambassador Spock once said that 'one should mourn the loss of life only if that life has been wasted.' " T'Lor sighed. "Jup died to save everyone else. I honor his courage and loyalty."

Kathryn instantly changed her opinion about T'Lor's potential as a diplomat. The Vulcan girl could not have chosen better words to convey her sympathies to a Klingon.

Without speaking, Thorn turned to stare out over the green valley so far below. Then he tilted his head back and emitted a powerful, spine-tingling howl.

Fiona screeched and dove to skim the tops of the trees on the distant valley floor, as though bidding farewell to a friend.

Kathryn eased back off the ledge, leaving Thorn alone to grieve in his own way.

Following her back into the clearing, Endar took Jon aside and sat down with him on the thick moss.

Amazed, Kathryn watched as the Talarian tried to comfort the boy. Jon had experienced the *targ's* death and surprisingly, Endar seemed to sense that it might have lasting, harmful effects if Jon didn't talk about it. Almost, but not quite, as surprising, the normally withdrawn Betazoid seemed willing to talk.

Then Kathryn noticed T'Lor heading into the trees. *Choka!*

In their fright during the cat's charge and their despair over Jup's death, they had all forgotten about the *sehlat*. The other animals were tense and upset, but none of them was in danger. Choka had cried out just before the cat attacked and he was still missing, either hurt or dead somewhere in the forest. Kathryn ran to help T'Lor search.

"I do not think we should split up, Kathryn." T'Lor scanned the trees, her face a reserved, unemotional mask.

Kathryn was not fooled by the Vulcan's outward calm. T'Lor was frantic with worry. "You're right. There could be more of those big cats close by. Let's fan out a little and just keep each other in sight."

Nodding, T'Lor started to walk forward and stopped. "Did you hear that?"

"Yes! A whining. . . ." Kathryn listened, then pointed to the left. "This way." As they turned, the *sehlat* limped out of the shadows.

"Choka!" Smiling with open relief and delight, T'Lor ran to the *sehlat's* side and laughed as he nuzzled her face. "You're all right!"

"His foot's hurt," Kathryn said, coming up beside

them. She pretended not to notice the girl's momentary emotional lapse.

Quickly composing herself, T'Lor examined Choka's foot and pulled out a four-inch thorn that was embedded in his pad. "I have something to seal the wound in my kit. He'll be fine."

"I'm glad of that," Kathryn said as they walked back toward the clearing with Choka limping gamely between them. She didn't think she could stand losing another of the team's animals. She had become fonder of the ugly, bristle-haired Klingon *targ* than she realized.

When they came out of the woods, Kathryn and T'Lor found Thorn, Endar, and Jon checking all the other animals to make sure they were all right.

"Why did you howl like that, Thorn?" Jon asked as he fed Rayonica's left head a handful of dried bugs. Her other heads were on watch, nostrils flaring and eyes trained on the woods.

"It is a Klingon ritual that honors the death of a comrade," Thorn answered. "We howl to warn the dead that a warrior is about to arrive."

"And Jup was a great warrior." Kathryn smiled. "I'll miss him."

"We owe him our lives," Endar said solemnly.

Thorn nodded slightly and sighed. "I owe him more than that. I have always been afraid that I would disgrace myself when someone close to me died in battle."

Kathryn sensed an urgency in the Klingon's confession of his most dreaded fear. By telling them, he was cementing the bond Jup's loss had created among them.

"Now I know I can handle it." Drawing another deep breath, Thorn squared his shoulders. "But it is more important than ever to complete this mission successfully now. Success will honor Jup's memory."

"I agree," Kathryn said, "but that's not the only reason we have to finish on schedule. We have another problem."

Jon looked at her and squinted. His expression quickly shifted between joy and concern. "The beam-out!"

Kathryn glanced at him, suddenly aware that Jon had been reading her mind. "Yes. Exactly."

"We'll make it in time," Endar said confidently.

"Time isn't what I'm worried about," Kathryn explained. "This planet doesn't really have an ionized atmosphere to prevent using the *McMurray*'s transporters. Captain Holbrook should have beamed all of us out of here the moment that cat attacked."

Everyone stared at her, not understanding the implications.

"But he didn't," Kathryn continued, "and there's only one explanation I can think of for why we're still here."

Thorn frowned, puzzled. "Why?"

"We've been cut off from the ship."

Chapter

10

"We're on our own?" Jon asked. "Captain Holbrook doesn't know where we are or anything?"

Kathryn nodded. "I think so."

"It's the only conclusion that makes sense." T'Lor sat on the ground, cleaning the Choka's puncture wound.

"Yes." Thorn clenched his teeth. "Captain Holbrook would not have let Jup die if it could have been avoided."

Endar frowned slightly, but kept his thoughts to himself. Kathryn couldn't tell if he agreed or disagreed, but his stubborn determination to discount anything T'Lor or Jon or she had to say was wearing on her nerves.

"We must proceed to the beam-out location as planned." Finishing her first aid on Choka's paw, T'Lor stood up. "If Captain Holbrook is unable to monitor us, he doesn't know about the cat's attack or Jup's death. Therefore, *he* doesn't know that *we* know we're out of contact with the *McMurray*."

"And if the ship *doesn't* get communications and the transporters working," Jon added, "the transporter site is where Captain Holbrook will expect to find us. The ship will probably send a shuttle to pick us up, so we'd better be there."

Kathryn raised an impressed eyebrow. "That's excellent deduction, Jon."

The Betazoid boy blushed with a mischievous smile. "Actually, that's what all of *you* were thinking."

"You can read our minds now?" T'Lor asked curiously.

"Sorry." Jon wrinkled his nose apologetically. "Thorn reacted so strongly when Jup fell, it broke through the block I had or something. I promise I'll try to control myself."

Thorn scowled his most menacing Klingon scowl. "See that you do!"

Jon grinned. "Nice try, Thorn, but I *know* you're not really mad."

The Klingon laughed. "We must stay in contact when the mission is over, Jon Brezi. You will be a valuable ally."

"Don't you think we should get moving?" Endar asked.

"Yes," Kathryn said. "After we dismantle and load

the surveillance probe. We can't abandon the mission just because we've run into some difficulties."

Everyone agreed with that and they set to work freeing the mechanism from its hiding place. A flat piece of rock had been fitted into the ledge on top of it. Endar and Thorn pried it loose, exposing the probe so it could be lifted up and out. No one had to risk dangling over the edge of the cliff on a rope.

When the device was separated into parts and the parts stashed in everyone's saddlebags, the team hit the trail again. According to Thorn, they only had to make up fifteen minutes to be back on their tight but doable schedule.

That isn't going to be easy, Kathryn thought, sitting back in her saddle to balance Tango as he half-slid down a rocky incline. The terrain on the far side of the mountain was rougher and more hazardous than it was on the southern face. Putting the safety of themselves and the animals first, they lost more and more minutes as the afternoon moved steadily toward dusk.

They weren't worried about being stranded. A shuttle was sure to be waiting for them. However, if they were late, Captain Holbrook might dispatch a search party to look for them. They would have failed to complete the exercise, and no one was willing to accept failure. Resolved, they pushed on down the mountain into the night.

"We stop here," Thorn announced as the tired team rode into a narrow canyon. He beamed his flashlight toward rock walls and surveyed the ground. "The rock is smooth and we can build a fire."

Kathryn looked around and nodded. It was their best bet for a place to camp. They were now fifteen minutes ahead of schedule and the animals had been watered at a small stream an hour back. Sleeping on smooth rock wouldn't be pleasant, but it would be a lot more comfortable than sleeping on a bed of small stones. A campfire would not only ward off the mountain cold, it would warm their weary spirits, too.

Once the animals were unsaddled, rubbed down, and fed, Kathryn and Jon cleared the area of loose rocks and brush while Thorn, Endar, and T'Lor gathered wood for the fire. Scrub pines with bluish needles grew in spots along the base of the walls and in crags up the rock face.

Kathryn started as Jon looked up suddenly.

"Run!" T'Lor shouted from the darkness a short distance down the ravine. The sound of boots pounding against rock echoed off the canyon walls.

"What's happening?" Kathryn grabbed a rock and a heavy pine branch to use as weapons.

Jon grabbed the leather bag full of sandbats. "Rats! They're being chased by rats!"

"Rats?" Kathryn shuddered.

"Or something like that." Without hesitation, Jon opened the pouch and closed his eyes. Six quiet rocklike sandbats came to life instantly and streamed out of the bag on leathery ribbed wings.

Kathryn peered down the canyon. Thorn, Endar, and T'Lor raced toward them with a pack of giant ratlike creatures snapping at their heels. The air was filled with the sound of frenzied snarls and growls.

Ignoring the alien teenagers, the sandbats dive-bombed the vicious rodents. Endar, Thorn, and T'Lor stopped and turned when they realized the sharp-toothed horde was no longer scrambling around their feet. Flashlights flicked on and everyone trained the beams on the furious battle.

The stubby-tailed rats of Diehr IV jumped at the zooming sandbats, jaws snapping. The bats dove, buzzed, and rose to dive again on wings that were ten times the size of their small bodies. As the rodents turned tail and ran from the mini-monsters battering them in the dark, one of the rats sank its teeth into a wing.

"Teesha!" Jon screamed as the small bat squealed in pain and fright.

Kathryn sprang forward armed only with her rock and pine branch. The team was not going to lose another friend if she could help it. It was hard to see in the dim glow cast by the flashlights, and she hesitated. She didn't want to strike the bat by mistake.

The light brightened suddenly as Thorn ran up behind her. The rat was shaking the terrified bat, beating its delicate wings against the ground. Taking careful aim, Kathryn brought the stick down square on the rodent's back. It released the sandbat with a shriek, then whirled to face Kathryn with its needle-sharp teeth bared.

"Run or die, rat," Kathryn said evenly. "Those are your only two choices." She didn't want to kill the creature if it wasn't absolutely necessary.

The rat ran.

Thorn quickly stepped up and handed Kathryn the flashlight. The sandbat remained silent and unmoving as he gently picked it up and cradled it in his massive hands.

"Is it dead?" Kathryn whispered.

"No. I feel the heart beating. T'Lor will know what to do." Murmuring softly to the injured creature, Thorn hurried back to the others.

Endar quickly lit the fire as everyone gathered around the Vulcan. "Do all your rock-bats have names, Jon?"

Jon nodded, but he did not take his eyes off T'Lor and the wounded Teesha. The other five sandbats perched on a boulder behind him, looking like rocks sitting on a rock.

"The teeth only perforated the wing membrane," T'Lor said softly. As she finished applying an antiseptic to the bite, the sandbat curled back into a tight ball. "I think it's in shock, though. You must keep it warm."

"I will." Jon sighed as he took Teesha from T'Lor's hands and held it against his chest. "Thank you, T'Lor."

"You're welcome."

"We'll need more wood to keep the fire going." Endar looked down the dark canyon with a frown.

"The sandbats will go after those rat things the minute they smell them again," Jon said. "Don't worry, Endar."

"I won't." Endar almost smiled.

At least Jon's made an impression on the Talarian,

Kathryn thought, *but he's a boy*. Hoping Endar could set aside his culture's condescending and dismissive attitudes toward females was probably too much to ask.

By the time Thorn and Endar had stacked enough wood for the night, Kathryn and T'Lor had finished setting up camp. When Teesha's struggle to join its companions threatened to do more harm than the cold, Jon put it on the rock with the other sandbats. All six of them immediately scooted closer to the fire and the team settled down to eat.

"How come you didn't let them out of their bag before?" Thorn asked.

Jon shrugged. "They like privacy and were happier in the bag. Now they have a good reason to be out. They will guard us from the rats all night." Swallowing the last of his Deltan pudding, Jon cocked his head toward Kathryn. "What does 'Tango' mean?"

Kathryn sat back slightly. "Actually, it doesn't *mean* anything. The tango is an ancient Earth dance."

"A sacred ritual," Thorn stated solemnly.

"Not exactly. We do it for fun."

"Fun?" Thorn faked a shocked expression. "I did not know you serious Starfleet people did anything just because it's fun."

"Vulcans do not," T'Lor emphatically corrected him.

"Talarians dance only to honor the dead," Endar said.

Kathryn blinked. She had never thought of Klingons

doing anything for fun, either. "What do Klingons do?"

"Many things." Thorn licked his fingers, then tossed his empty flash-pack in the fire. "Personally, I like Klingon opera. But I'm curious about this Earth dance. You must show us."

"I've heard Klingon opera, Kathryn." A slight grimace disrupted T'Lor's calm expression. "A demonstration of this tango would be infinitely preferable."

It was another cultural gap Kathryn had an opportunity to bridge, but not at the expense of her dignity. Recalling another of her father's archaic sayings, she begged off. "I'm afraid it takes two to tango."

"I'll tango with you!" Jon jumped to his feet, his eyes bright with enthusiasm.

"I'm not a very good dancer," Kathryn said desperately.

"I don't think I am, either." Jon laughed. "I've never tried!"

"Come on, Kathryn!" Thorn prodded. "We have the probe and we're ahead of schedule. We should do *something* to celebrate!"

Sighing, Kathryn stood up and brushed the dust off her uniform. She suspected Thorn wanted something to distract him from thinking about Jup. And now that Jon had come out of his shell, she did not feel comfortable rejecting his efforts to be sociable. Not even if it meant making a fool of herself for a few minutes.

Clasping the younger boy's right hand in her left, Kathryn positioned her other hand on his waist and his hand on hers. Then she bestowed her own most menacing glare on their audience. "I'll get *my* revenge on the first one who laughs."

They all made an effort to look suitably grim.

"Ready?" Kathryn smiled at Jon, then turned sideways and straightened her arm. Singing the rhythm, she steered the awkward boy forward with dramatic sweeping steps, then reversed their position and swooped back. "Taaa-daaa da-da-dah. Taaa-dah da-da-dah . . ."

Within seconds, T'Lor was tapping her foot and Thorn was bellowing along in a grating, baritone voice. Fiona and Choka watched in animal bewilderment. Endar collapsed in a heap of uncontrollable, amused laughter that sent Fooz scurrying into his hair. As soon as Jon got the hang of the movements, he began singing the rhythmic tune, too.

Self-conscious but delighted that everyone was enjoying themselves, Kathryn threw herself into the dance. She dipped, paused, and turned with an increasing energy that Jon matched stride for stride. She was taken totally by surprise when she stumbled over a rock on the edge of the campsite. Jon let go as she lost her balance and fell backward in the dirt.

"Are you all right, Kathryn?"

Kathryn did not move or answer. Her fall had aroused a snake sleeping by the rocks. Two feet to her right, the wedge-shaped head of the coiled reptile swayed, poised to strike. Venom dripped from its lethal fangs.

Jon backed up slowly. Realizing something was

wrong, T'Lor, Endar, and Thorn stood up. They hesitated when the boy motioned them to be quiet and still.

"What's going on?" Endar whispered.

"A snake," Jon hissed softly.

Kathryn did not dare move her head. She didn't dare twitch for fear the slightest movement would prompt the snake to attack. But out of the corner of her eye she saw the Talarian edge closer and stoop to place Fooz on the ground. The huge, black spider crept forward.

Kathryn's blood turned cold.

The snake's venom might kill her in seconds.

But another danger was moving toward her on eight black nine-inch legs. The Talarian hook spider's poisonous bite was fatal, too.

Had Endar sent Fooz to save her?

Or to make sure the Talarians had one less Starfleet officer to worry about in the future?

Chapter

11

Kathryn's instincts told her to trust the Talarian. In spite of Endar's animosity toward the Federation and his lack of respect for women, he was honorable. He would not deliberately hurt anyone who had done him no harm.

Remaining perfectly still, Kathryn watched the snake. It hissed and darted its head forward, then back, toying with her. Her heart fluttered, but she did not flinch when Fooz crawled over her outstretched legs.

The snake struck suddenly.

But it was not fast enough.

The hook spider leaped and grabbed the snake behind the head in his powerful mandibles. Throwing

the reptile to the ground, the spider hung on until the snake's long, twisting body stopped struggling.

Kathryn didn't move until Endar appeared and scooped the spider into his arms. When the Talarian held out his hand to help her up, she took it.

"Did the snake bite you?" Endar asked.

Kathryn shook her head. "No, thanks to Fooz. And you."

"We couldn't afford to lose another valuable member of the team."

Kathryn nodded and smiled as the others rushed forward to express their relief and praise the spider. Endar meant no insult by comparing her to the lost *targ*. It was a sincere compliment. She accepted it graciously and without additional comment, knowing how difficult it was for the Talarian to accept a girl as an equal.

Anxious to get an early start, the team bedded down for the night with Fooz, Fiona, Choka, and the sandbats watching over the camp.

Although she was exhausted, Kathryn's mind reeled with several realizations that kept her awake.

Jup's heroic death had broken down the barriers that had kept everyone operating as separate entities rather than as a team. They had finally recognized the one thing they all had in common—their concern and respect for the animals. And that had made them realize that they respected and cared about one another, too.

Thorn's firm belief that Captain Holbrook would have saved the *targ* if possible was proof that the Klingon Empire and the Federation might someday learn to *really* trust each other. Thorn would become a Klingon leader committed to making that happen.

The positive, long-range effects of Jup's death were staggering. If a *targ* could have such a potentially powerful impact on the galaxy, how much difference could one human girl make? *A lot,* Kathryn decided. As a Starfleet officer with an understanding of different alien viewpoints and motives, social customs and beliefs, she could make a *big* difference in a lot of little ways.

I already have, Kathryn realized with a glance at Endar, who had chosen to sleep on the ground. T'Lor's medicine had completely healed the hives and he didn't want to expose himself to tree bark again. The Talarian had finally overcome his ingrained conviction that all females were helpless and all Federation citizens were enemies. It wasn't likely the ongoing hostilities between the Talarian homeworld and the Federation would end, but maybe someday the change in Endar's rigid attitude would help him peacefully resolve a situation involving Starfleet.

And she would never again make the mistake of judging people based on cultural or political misconceptions, either. If treated fairly and honestly, individuals could learn to work together and respect one another, even like one another, regardless of their governments' politics or personal differences of opinion. Diversity was the team's strength.

Kathryn dozed off knowing that they would succeed or fail together. But she also knew that they were unanimously determined to succeed—for Captain Hol-brook, for Jup, and because it was a matter of team pride.

Everyone was up before dawn. They were packed and heading out as the golden sun of Diehr IV rose over the mountain—an hour ahead of Thorn's calculated schedule. However, it soon became apparent that the extra time would be spent solving more unexpected problems.

The only thing we can predict is that the unpredictable will *happen,* Kathryn thought as the team stood on the bank of a narrow, raging river. Shammi, T'Lor's Andorian *zabathu,* refused to go near it. The desert animal did not balk at drinking from or jumping over quiet streams, but the whitewater rapids terrified her.

Thorn and Endar rode back from scouting the river in both directions.

"There's no easy way across and no way around to the west," Thorn said.

"Nor to the east, either." Endar scowled thoughtfully. "We have to cross here or the mission is over."

"There's got to be a way!" Jon's awakened ability to read intelligent thoughts had revealed that his older companions not only worried about him, they cared about him, too. Knowing they valued his ability to communicate with animals and considered him to be an important member of the team had made the Betazoid obsessively determined to arrive at the beam-out point on time.

"Is it the sound of the water that frightens

Shammi?" T'Lor asked the Betazoid. "Or something else?"

Jon frowned and closed his eyes to touch the *zabathu*'s mind. When he opened his eyes, he shook his head in frustration. "I can't tell. She's too scared."

"I have an idea," Kathryn said.

"Let's hear it." Endar looked at her evenly.

"Humans blindfold horses to get them out of burning barns," Kathryn explained. "It works because they can't see the flames. They're so used to trusting the people leading them, they follow."

Thorn glanced at the Vulcan. "What do you think, T'Lor? Will it work?"

"We won't know until we try." T'Lor calmly ripped the sleeve off her tunic and tied it over the *zabathu*'s eyes.

"It might help if you and I flank her as we're going across, Kathryn," Endar said. "Then she won't be able to move sideways."

"Good idea." Kathryn twisted in her saddle to look at Jon. "Jon should follow behind so Rayonica is downwind."

"She's accustomed to Hov nej being in front of her." T'Lor took Shammi's halter out of her saddlebag and fitted it over the bridle. She handed the lead rope to Thorn and mounted up.

Kathryn approved. If the Klingon had to pull to get the *zabathu* moving, he wouldn't be yanking on the bit and hurting Shammi's mouth. And T'Lor would still have the reins if the *zabathu* happened to break free and bolt. Nodding to Endar, Kathryn moved

Tango to Shammi's left side while the Talarian placed the *t'stayan* on the right.

Tightening his grip on the rope, Thorn urged the *sark* into the cascading water. Shammi planted her feet, her ears flicking back and forth uncertainly. T'Lor kicked and Thorn yanked. The *zabathu* leaped into the water and froze. As strong as Thorn was, he could not get her moving again until Jon eased the serpent forward. Rayonica hissed and butted Shammi in the rump with her middle head. The left and right heads gently nipped her flanks. The *zabathu*'s instinctive fear of the 'saur was greater than her dread of the water. She bounded forward, almost colliding with Hov nej before Thorn got the heavy *sark* moving. The team sprang up the opposite bank in perfect formation.

Kathryn felt a rush of satisfaction. Even Endar grinned, pleased with how they had conquered a seemingly impossible problem.

They did not waste time congratulating themselves. Encouraged because the river was safely behind them, they pushed on. Even the animals seemed energized, as though they knew the end of the journey was near.

Maybe they do, Kathryn thought as they rode over the spongy, moss-covered ground of another forest. *Maybe Jon told them.*

T'Lor's medicine had done wonders for Choka's paw. He continued circling the group, running in and out of the trees with no sign of a limp. Fooz nestled around Endar's neck, content to doze, and the sand-bats were quiet in their bag. Above the trees, Fiona shrieked, anxious for the team to emerge into the open again.

The terrain became less rugged as the hours passed and they descended the mountain. Thorn assured them that if nothing else happened to slow them down, they would enter the designated clearing with a half hour to spare.

Kathryn didn't say so, but she had become all too aware that the Chance Factor was not likely to let them off that easily. It was constant and inescapable. She was not being pessimistic. Expecting the unexpected was the only way to be prepared to deal with it quickly and effectively.

Up ahead, Thorn paused and then abruptly backed up the *sark*. "Quicksand!"

Everyone stopped dead as the Klingon consulted his map.

"Is there a way around it?" T'Lor asked.

Thorn nodded. "If we go east, we'll hit slightly higher land. It'll take extra time, but we'll still be okay."

"Better to be late than sucked into that quagmire," Endar said.

"We won't be late." Thorn tapped the map. "After this, the terrain is level meadow and woodlands. We can pick up our pace."

Steering wide of the quicksand bog, the team carefully picked their way toward the higher elevation. Kathryn noticed that a peculiar short bush with twisted branches and long spikes instead of leaves grew along the perimeter of the quagmire. Within a few minutes, she realized that the ground to the right of the bushes remained solid. After Thorn confirmed that fact, they urged their animals into a steady jog without fear of stumbling into the deadly muck.

Leaving the bog behind, they emerged onto a grassy meadow rimmed by trees and dotted with colorful yellow and purple flowers. Thorn found an animal trail that allowed them to cross the open space at a brisk canter. Being able to see the bare ground reduced the risk of one of their animals stepping into a hidden hole that could snap a leg.

Fiona soared overhead, content to ride the winds, and Choka ran beside T'Lor's *zabathu.*

Tensions seemed to mount as they drew closer to their destination. Kathryn was gripped by a nervous anticipation that made her extra cautious and alert. They were so close to completing the mission on time, she could not bring herself to relax. They were not done yet and something could still go wrong.

The path curved and Hov nej plowed through a dense thicket of red-leafed bushes. A swarm of large winged insects erupted from the bushes with a shrill, whistling screech.

Tango shied, but Kathryn's grip was sure and she clung to the saddle. Ahead of her, the *sark* kept going and the *zabathu* bucked. Rayonica, startled by the insects and wary of Shammi's back hooves, skidded to a halt and unseated Jon. The boy yelped as he slid off the serpent's back and landed on the ground. Somehow, he managed to hold up the leather bag so his sandbats weren't squashed under him.

Disoriented and startled, the serpent bolted back across the meadow.

Kathryn didn't have time to discuss her actions. The horse was the only animal fast enough to catch the speeding dinosaur. Reining Tango around, she urged him into a gallop. He took off with the unbelievable burst of speed the quarter horse had been bred for. Kathryn called back over her shoulder, "Keep going! I'll meet you at the beam-out site!"

Thorn waved as he dismounted and grabbed Jon's arm as the boy started to run after Kathryn. The struggling Betazoid was no match for the Klingon. Thorn boosted the boy onto the *sark*'s back, swung up behind him, and pressed on toward the transporter site.

Rising off the saddle and hunching over Tango's neck, Kathryn desperately hoped there were no holes hidden in the tall grass as she charged after Rayonica.

Caution was not an option if she wanted to save Jon's Sehgal serpent from a terrifying and agonizing death.

The panicked lizard was running straight toward the quicksand bog.

Chapter

12

Keeping her eye on Rayonica, Kathryn listened to the steady cadence of Tango's pounding hooves. The 'saur was closing on the line of spiked bushes with twisted branches that marked the edge of the deadly bog. The sturdy little horse was gaining, but not fast enough. She wasn't going to catch Rayonica in time.

Kathryn couldn't bear the thought of losing the dinosaur. The Sehgal serpent was more than a riding animal to Jon. She was his best friend.

Overhead, the Baneriam hawk screeched.

Desperate, Kathryn looked up. The bird was flying directly over Rayonica. Giant lizards were not on the hawk's normal menu and the bird's talons wouldn't do more than scratch the dinosaur's thick hide. It was a long shot that didn't have much chance of working, but it was the only chance she had.

"Hunt, Fiona! Hunt!" Kathryn pointed to the serpent.

The hawk darted forward on magnificent wings, then suddenly circled back. Screeching again, the bird dove directly toward Rayonica from the front.

The unexpected attack from the sky shattered the serpent's blind panic. Three heads snapped up in alarm. Putting on the brakes, Rayonica skidded as the hawk skimmed over her back. The lizard's side brushed the spiked bushes as she whirled and ran back toward Kathryn.

Slowing Tango, Kathryn watched as Fiona dove a second time. The serpent also slowed, its heads weaving from side to side in confusion.

"Fiona! Break!"

Rayonica came to a shaking halt as the hawk broke off a third attack run and soared back into the sky.

Bringing Tango down to a walk, Kathryn cautiously approached the winded lizard. Unlike the other team animals and the thoroughbred back at the Academy, the quarter horse was calmly tolerant of the reptile-like dinosaur. Stopping a few feet away, Kathryn dismounted. Tango waited quietly as she eased up to Rayonica and gently took the reins. Six eyes watched her warily as she slipped the leathers over the serpent's center head. Speaking softly, she chanced scratching the left head's chin. Rayonica *whuff*ed and obediently followed as Kathryn slowly walked back to

the horse. Tango snorted as she swung back into the saddle, but remained calm.

Holding the lizard's reins in one hand, Kathryn squeezed Tango into a walk. The horse started forward, totally accepting the presence of the dinosaur lumbering by his side. He did not even flinch when the left head nuzzled his neck. Kathryn patted Rayonica's snout and grinned.

The rest of the team had already passed into the woods on the far side of the meadow. Even though Rayonica and Tango were tired after their mad gallop, Kathryn pushed them into a trot. Both animals were fit and bred for endurance. There would be time to rest after they reached the transporter site. Kathryn did not doubt that they'd get there, but if she didn't arrive on time, the mission would fail. She was not going to let the team down.

Finding the animal track again, Kathryn urged Tango into a canter. The serpent loped beside them without fighting the tug on the reins. Kathryn slowed down to a jog once she entered the woods and followed the tracks the team had left in the soft dirt. When she emerged from the trees, she found herself in another open meadow. There was no visible trail to follow.

With less than half an hour left before the deadline, Kathryn did not want to waste time finding her way by the map. But she would be hopelessly lost if she didn't. As she reached into her saddlebag, a piercing howl sounded up ahead.

Choka bounded out of the tall grass, yelped, then

whirled and bounded away again. Pressing Tango into a slow canter, Kathryn followed the *sehlat* T'Lor had sent to guide her.

When Kathryn entered the clearing where the team was waiting, she was met with a resounding cheer!

There was no shuttle standing by to retrieve them.

Jon broke free of T'Lor's comforting arm and rushed forward to throw his arms around all of Rayonica's rough, green necks. The serpent flicked out her center tongue to tickle his ear. "You got her! T'Lor said you would. Thank you, Kathryn."

T'Lor inclined her head at Kathryn, almost but not quite showing her relief at Rayonica's safe return.

"You're welcome, Jon." Urging Tango back into a walk to keep him moving until he cooled down, Kathryn looked at Thorn. "What time is it?"

"Two minutes to go." Thorn raised a victorious fist and laughed out loud.

Endar smiled. "Looks like you picked the right horse after all, Kathryn Janeway. Nobody else could have saved Jon's serpent."

"Fiona helped." Looking skyward, Kathryn called the hawk back as Thorn started the countdown. She stopped and slid out of the saddle when he reached five.

". . . four, three, two, one." Thorn looked up.

Everyone held their breath.

No one disappeared in a dazzling swirl of transporter light.

Another minute passed, and another. Kathryn

walked Tango while the others fussed over their animals and gear.

"Do you think we're stranded?" Jon asked.

Kathryn opened her mouth to respond, then felt the prickling sensation as her molecules began to phase.

They had made it.

Kathryn was greeted by the transporter chief when she materialized on the cargo bay pad.

"Captain Holbrook will be along soon," the woman said.

Nodding, Kathryn set about taking care of Tango and Fiona while the others were beamed onto the *McMurray*. Everyone was excited. They had accomplished what they had set out to do against the odds and in spite of the Chance Factor.

The cargo bay doors opened the moment they finished bedding down the animals, and Captain Holbrook walked in with a huge smile plastered on his face. He stopped before the table where the surveillance probe parts had been placed and nodded in approval.

"Excellent! Starfleet has already informed me that I'll be getting funding for additional research. And I've notified all the proper people on your various homeworlds that you're all to be commended on a difficult job well done."

Kathryn grinned as Endar slapped her on the back and Thorn hugged Jon. T'Lor sedately shook the captain's hand, then grunted as Choka nudged her from behind, looking for a pat on the head.

The captain glanced at Kathryn. "Including Commander Brannon. Your position at the Academy is secure, Kathryn. If you want it."

"There's nothing else in the whole galaxy I want more." Kathryn felt a rush of joy that was diminished only by a strange sadness because the adventure was over. She would miss her new friends.

Her thoughts seemed to be mirrored in the alien faces around her. As difficult as getting to know and appreciate one another had been, the parting at the end of the trip back to Earth would be harder. Good friends you could trust and depend on were not easy to find.

"You should be especially proud of the animals," Captain Holbrook said. "They all proved to be invaluable. Although, I've learned that the animals can only be as effective as the people who handle them."

Everyone just nodded. Kathryn's thoughts instantly turned to the dead *targ*. It was a loss they all felt very deeply.

"Wait a minute." Captain Holbrook frowned as he scanned the stalls. "Someone's missing."

"Jup." Thorn's eyes filled with pride. "He gave his life to save us from a predator that attacked unexpectedly."

"Yes, I know." Captain Holbrook grinned.

Everyone gasped in surprise as a squealing, grunting *targ* suddenly burst through the cargo bay doors and raced to Thorn.

"Jup! You're alive!" Thorn laughed as he stooped down to embrace the ecstatic, squirming *targ*.

Even T'Lor's eyes brightened with delight.

THE CHANCE FACTOR

"We beamed him out before he hit the ground," the captain explained. "And we transported the Diehr Four cat to another location on the planet."

"We thought we had been cut off from the ship," Kathryn said.

Captain Holbrook winked. "Yes, I know."

Kathryn laughed. She didn't know if Captain Holbrook had taken drastic action to save his study mission or to help the team members come to terms with themselves and one another. It didn't matter. It had worked.

For herself, Kathryn looked toward the future with enthusiastic anticipation and confidence. She didn't know where her Starfleet career would take her, but she knew she could handle the ever-present Chance Factor regardless of how many curves it threw at her.

Even if it threw her into the farthest, unknown reaches of the galaxy!

About the Authors

Diana G. Gallagher and Martin R. Burke are married and live in Minnesota with three dogs, three cats, and a cranky parrot. When Diana's not writing, she likes to read, walk the dogs, and look for cool stuff at garage sales for their grandsons, Jonathan, Alan, and Joseph. Marty spends his spare time reading, jogging, and cruising the Net.

Diana and Marty are musicians who perform traditional and original Irish and American folk music at coffeehouses and conventions around the country. Marty sings and plays the twelve-string guitar and banjo. In addition to singing backup harmonies, Diana plays rhythm guitar and a round Celtic drum called a *bodhran*.

Marty and Diana have other coauthored writing projects in progress, and Marty is currently working on an original novel. A Hugo Award–winning artist, Diana is best known for her series *Woof: The House Dragon*. Her first adult novel, *The Alien Dark*, appeared in 1990. In addition to other STAR TREK novels for intermediate readers, she has written many books in other series published by Minstrel Books, including *The Secret World of Alex Mack, Are You Afraid of the Dark,* and *The Mystery Files of Shelby Woo*. She is currently working on original young adult novels for the Archway Paperback series *Sabrina, the Teenage Witch*.

A Special Event!

**Celebrate the Klingon™ Day of Honor
with Worf and Alexander!**

STAR TREK
DEEP SPACE NINE®

#11
DAY OF HONOR
HONOR BOUND

To lose one's honor is the greatest loss of all...

By Diana G. Gallagher

Coming mid-September '97

A MINSTREL® BOOK

Published by Pocket Books

1393-01

Sometimes, it takes a kid to solve a good crime....

Original stories based on the hit Nickelodeon show!

#1 A Slash in the Night
by Alan Goodman

#2 Takeout Stakeout
By Diana G. Gallagher

#3 Hot Rock
by John Peel

#4 Rock 'n' Roll Robbery
by Lydia C. Marano and David Cody Weiss

(Coming in mid-October 1997)

To find out more about *The Mystery Files of Shelby Woo* or any other Nickelodeon show, visit Nickelodeon Online on America Online (Keyword: NICK) or send e-mail (NickMailDD@aol.com).

A MINSTREL BOOK

Published by Pocket Books

1338-02